GUARD

HARD HIT #11

CHARITY PARKERSON

–Warning: This book is intended for readers over the age of 18.

Editor: Hercules Editing & Consultants
ISBN-13: 978-1-946099-24-2

 Created with Vellum

INTRODUCTION

THE ONLY THING WORSE THAN SUFFERING A
BROKEN HEART IS BEING FORCED TO PRETEND IT
NEVER HAPPENED.

For two years, Mara kept a secret. She was in love with two members of her security team—Landon and Early. As an actress, she's always in the spotlight. Keeping her reputation intact is more important than anything. Until the day came that she no longer cared. Loving Early and Landon meant too much to keep hiding. That was the day she lost them.

For a year, Mara has suffered in silence. The world doesn't see her loss. They don't know she's broken. She's never been more alone. Her downhill spiral forces Kieran Steele to step in, sending her someone to watch over her. Someone every bit as shattered. Now only time will tell if a bucketful of secrets will draw them closer or tear them apart.

Meanwhile, something is happening with Henley, causing problems in his marriage with Kieran. As Kieran struggles to find the key to save their relationship, Henley pulls farther away.

I have to send a huge "thank you" to award-winning producer, John Foutz from Foutz Studios, for answering all my research questions about movie production and set life. Your friendship is beyond priceless.

CHAPTER ONE

Mara seriously considered sneaking out on her own, making a liquor run, and then hiding in her bedroom for the rest of the night. Fortunately, some sane part of her brain took over, reminding her she'd like to stay in one piece. Most days, being a celebrity was amazing. The trade-off was she never went anywhere without her full-time security team. She recognized she had more than most —was blessed and all that shit. Tonight, it didn't feel like it. She wanted to crawl out of her skin. Something felt off. She was tired of hiding in her home, shielding her personal life. Most of all, she was sick of hiding behind a line of fake relationships to camouflage reality. It was all for the benefit of others. She wasn't ashamed. Instead of giving in to temptation, disappearing under the cover of darkness, and risking ending up tied up in some freak's basement, Mara tried sneaking downstairs to grab a bottle of vodka. She'd hoped to grab it and run away to be alone before Landon and Early realized she was still home. Her hopes were dashed upon the rocks as soon as her fingers curled around the bottle's neck.

"Got stood up again, huh?" Landon called out, freezing Mara in her tracks.

For a moment, she stood still, foolishly hoping he wasn't talking to her. She snuck a glance his way. Dark eyes met her gaze. Mara blew out a sigh. "It's Friday night, isn't it? Isn't it par for the course for me to get stood up?"

Landon shook his head and tossed his cards down on the table. She'd hoped his poker game would keep him too preoccupied to notice her presence. Not only had Mara been wrong, now both players watched her expectantly. Their eyes were night and day—Early's were as blue as the sky on a summer's day. Landon's were so dark she'd damn near call them pitch black. They always reflected the light of the room, capturing her gaze. Tonight was no different. Mara couldn't move.

"Why haven't you dumped this guy yet?"

It was a fair question. She'd been fake-dating Sean Pearson for six months. He'd shown up for a total of four scheduled dates in that length of time. Mara would like to claim she knew how busy the man was. After all, being one of the biggest names in rock didn't leave much time for anything else. She'd equally like to say their schedules were constantly clashing, since being an actress took up most of her time. The truth was something altogether different.

Mara tugged at her short nightgown, feeling more exposed than she'd care to admit. She'd made up her mind about a few things recently. Unfortunately, she hadn't discussed them with Landon and Early yet. "Seems nuts to have to dump someone I'm not really dating."

Early smiled. Her beautiful dimples came out to play. She cast Landon a devilish glance. "Sounds to me like she's trying to say she's a free woman."

Landon's heated gaze traveled from Mara's toes to her face. "You're not a free woman."

It took every ounce of Mara's strength not to press her hand to her stomach as the butterflies stirred. No. She wasn't free. Sean meant nothing to her, but Early and Landon—they were everything.

Landon pushed the empty chair at the table out with his foot. "You should join us then, since you're free to play." There was something dark in the man's tone. It was a hint of something unnamed. Mara had been noticing it more and more as of late. Her nipples hardened at the promise behind his words.

While still clinging to her bottle, Mara shuffled closer. Most people didn't hang out, playing cards with their security team. Of course, Landon and Early didn't really work for her, and they were so much more to her heart. "Will we be playing poker?"

"Yes," Early answered before Landon could.

Mara winced. "I'm not good at that."

Cheshire grins stretched their faces, but Landon was the one who spoke first. "You should never admit to being bad at poker, especially when the stakes are high."

"I have deeper pockets," Mara said, wincing as the words left her mouth.

"You're wearing less clothes," Early said just as fast.

So it was like that. Her mouth went dry. Mara wouldn't play the idiot. She sat down. The pair watched her every reaction with matching hungry gazes. Mara twisted off the vodka's cap and turned the bottle up. The alcohol burned her throat and gut. She didn't care. Mara needed liquid courage. The pair wanted to play tonight. Mara had something she needed to say.

Landon shuffled the cards. Early watched her. "Did

Sean really stand you up or did you cancel on him?"

Mara's brow furrowed in confusion at Early's question. "Why would you ask?"

Early flipped her long blonde curls over her shoulder as she sat forward, holding Mara's gaze. "See, Landon and I have a bet going. He thinks Sean's a prick who keeps standing you up. I think Sean's a loser who can't eat pussy, so you keep canceling on him to stay home with me."

To buy some time, Mara turned up the bottle again while pressing her thighs together. Liquid heat rushed to the apex of her thighs just hearing Early talk about eating pussy. She couldn't deny Early had an awesome mouth. "What's the bet up to now?" Mara asked around the burn in her throat.

"A hundred," Landon grunted as he tossed cards in their direction.

The alcohol hit Mara's brain. "Hmm," she hummed. "Maybe I'll wait until you're up to two hundred before answering."

Mara glanced between them before turning the bottle up once more. Early and Landon exchanged glances but didn't press. Instead, they picked up their cards and eyed them in silence. Mara did the same. She blinked at the three aces and a king in her hand, wondering if Landon had slipped her a good hand for some reason all his own.

"How are we doing this?" Mara asked while trying not to show her excitement over the prospect of winning. "Do we get chips or something?"

"We have our own set of rules," Landon said. "The losers of each hand have to draw a card. The person with the lowest card has to remove one item of clothing of the winner's choosing."

"Sounds legit," Mara said, taking another swig.

Early chewed her bottom lip while staring at her hand. Mara couldn't stop watching her. Early slid two facedown cards Landon's way. He gave her two more. The woman's expression never changed. Landon's eyebrows rose in question. Mara shook her head. She was happy with her hand. At Landon's nod, they each showed their hand. Early had a handful of nothing. Landon had two pair. Mara beamed. She'd won.

"Draw," she ordered, mentally rubbing her hands together. Mara loved to win.

They each drew a card. Landon a seven. Early a two. A smile that felt wicked even to Mara stretched her lips. Early's stare dared Mara to make the most of her win. After glancing under the table and assessing how much clothing Early wore, Mara made her decision. She'd ease into this.

"I want your shoe."

Early snorted but dutifully kicked off one shoe. The sound hardened Mara's nipples to the point of painful. Everything about Early had always turned her on. Landon pushed the cards her way to shuffle. She cut them and did her best to mix them up again before tossing them in Landon and Early's direction. This time, Mara didn't have shit. Only two cards matched. She exchanged three of them, hoping for better odds. No luck. Landon and Early both traded a few as well. Neither of them gave away a single hint as to their chances of winning. Once they'd done all they could do, they showed their hand once more. Early had a straight. Landon had four of kind. Mara's stomach muscles clenched as she drew a card. She drew a jack. Her muscles relaxed. Landon drew a king. Her heart slammed against the wall of her chest. Too late, she realized she wasn't wearing much. Early's expression said she wouldn't take the same mercy on Mara as Mara had on her.

"Panties," Early said, wiggling her fingers, waiting for Mara to hand them over. Since the choice had been between her nightgown or panties, Mara couldn't decide if she was relieved or not. Either way, she lost a key article of clothing. While keeping her lower half hidden by the table, Mara wiggled out of her underwear before handing the scrap of lace over. Early's eyes turned devilish as her fingers closed around the material. Mara turned her bottle up. There was no way Early missed how wet those panties were.

Early played the dealer next. This time around, Mara lost again but won the draw. Landon lost his shirt. She'd seen the man's golden brown and muscular chest hundreds of times. Tonight, Mara was barely holding it together. There was too much sexiness in one room. Too much heat between players. The alcohol in Mara's blood was soaking her brain. Instead of making her forget her worries, it reminded Mara of all the nights they'd spent twisted together—straining. She kept breathing through her nose, trying not to demand they stop this game.

Somehow, Mara hung on to her single article of clothing for three more hands until Landon won it. Mara slipped the satin material over her head and held it out to him. She kept her head held high. After all, they'd seen her nude hundreds of times. Matching hungry gazes eyed her body. It was her turn to deal. She shuffled as if she wasn't on display. Once again, she had nothing, and no clothes left to lose. If she lost this hand, her debt might be more than she could afford. After all, both Landon and Early were sexual deviants. Early won the hand. Landon won the draw.

Mara met Early's gaze. "I've already lost everything."

Early shook her head. Her lips turned up in an evil smile. "Not everything."

Mara's pussy soaked the chair. She licked her lips, refusing to back down. "Name your price." Even to her ears, the words sounded like a dare. Mara couldn't help it. She wanted to blame the alcohol for making her weak. Mara knew the truth—their love had made her weak long ago.

"I should go to bed," Mara said before Early could say anything Mara couldn't turn down.

"We should," Early agreed. "All of us. Together," she added.

Mara snuck a glance at Landon, curious about his thoughts on the matter. The heat meeting her stare nearly blasted her from her chair. His gaze dropped, eyeing her nude body before meeting her stare once more. Mara licked her parched lips. She'd never been more turned on or thankful for having skipped another fake date.

She stood. Mara fucking wanted everything their gazes offered. She wanted them with a crippling desire she couldn't control. They were seated and staring at her nude body, hungry and waiting for permission to feast. Mara fought the urge to press her hand to her mound and ease the pulsations. Her inner thighs were slick with her juices.

"Are you running out on your debt here?" Early asked, sounding calm and nowhere near as affected as Mara.

"No. You never named your price."

Early's mouth lifted in one corner. "Okay. Here it is—did you cancel on Sean or did he stand you up?"

"I cancelled."

Early nodded. "Why?"

Mara shifted, feeling exposed for the first time. As much as they needed to talk, Mara was scared. "I've already met your price."

Without a word, Landon stood, as if calling an end to their game. Mara couldn't look away from his intense stare as he moved in her direction. She was forced to tilt her chin back to hold his gaze when he came to stand over her. He slipped the nightgown over her head, leaving Mara no other choice than to lift her arms and let him dress her like a child. His thumbs brushed her hardened nipples as he smoothed the material over them. A gasp escaped before Mara could call it back. The satin slid down her body, falling into place. Landon didn't move away. Without warning, he swept Mara off her feet, stealing her breath. Before her mind came to terms with the change in position, Landon sat her on the edge of the table, coming to stand between her knees. Mara's tongue wouldn't work. All she could do was stare into his dark eyes.

"Why did you cancel?" Landon's question came out sounding deep, low, and sexy. Mara sucked in a sharp breath at the open lust in his tone. She was hyper aware of her hands resting on his waist. His body felt ridiculously tight and hard. Everything took on a surreal edge. "Tell me," Landon said, refusing to back down.

"I don't want to hide any longer." The words burst from Mara without her permission—like they'd been waiting on the edge of her tongue for the past two years.

Landon's expression transformed, shutting her out. "What?"

Mara took a breath. Even to her ears, it sounded shaky. "People come out all the time, Landon. I'm not saying I'll call the press tomorrow and announce our relationship, but if rumors start..." Mara shrugged.

With a small shake of his head, Landon flashed a sad smile. "It's not fair for you to taunt us with a life we'll never have." Landon's voice grew stronger. "How dare you make us question if you're acting—if this is improv and we're your test audience?" Mara didn't know how to react.

She'd never heard Landon sound so angry or seen his mood change so quickly. Mara couldn't keep up. "How dare you say something like that when it's all a game to you? It's our job to be with you. We're disposable. If you do this, no one will ever hire us again, and I just now got back into acting."

Mara's eyes and nose stung. Her lungs burned as if she'd been running a marathon. She couldn't tear her gaze away from his anger. "Being with me won't hurt you career. People come out all the time," Mara repeated, because she had no other argument other than her love. Right now, she wasn't sure that mattered much.

"You're cruel."

Mara drew back, feeling like she'd been slapped. She cared about them—more than they'd ever know. The burning behind her eyes increased. She'd never felt more exposed. Her throat wouldn't work. She couldn't defend herself. Landon didn't seem to need her words. He had plenty.

"Yeah, people come out all the time. They come out as gay," Landon roared, backing away from her and leaving her feeling exposed on the edge of the table. "How many people do you know who've come out with a relationship like ours? Exactly zero," Landon said without waiting for Mara's answer. "This might not ruin you, but it would cast a shadow over everything you do. All your charity work. Your domestic violence intervention program. Everything, Mara. No one will care about the good you do. All anyone will talk about is what you do in bed with Early and me. All anyone will talk about is how I broke into acting because I'm fucking you."

An unexpected burst of anger ran through Mara. "So you'd rather stay a secret? You want to live the rest of your life fearing an accidental brush of hands—too long of a lingering glance?"

"I didn't say that."

Landon's hard gaze made Mara's chest hurt. "What are you saying?"

Landon's chest expanded as he took a deep breath. Mara held hers, bracing for his next words. "I'm saying, I think maybe we should stop. We never meant for you to get this attached. I'm saying..." Landon calmed. It was almost eerie. As if he'd come to a decision that had been wearing on him. "The studio offered me another job in LA. I'm leaving in three weeks. For good."

Mara glanced Early's way, needing to see her reaction. She didn't look surprised. Early had known this was coming. Mara didn't know how she felt about that beyond the hurt—more alone than ever, perhaps. It seemed she was the outsider. Mara slid from the table and headed for the stairs without looking back. Neither tried to stop her. When Mara reached the bedroom she'd shared with Landon and Early the past two years, she closed the door, shutting herself away from the secrets they'd kept. From the beginning, she'd always known Early and Landon confided things in each other they kept from her. Before today, Mara hadn't openly acknowledged to herself how much it hurt. All it had taken was for her to want things they didn't, and it ripped apart everything they'd shared. She didn't doubt for a moment wherever Landon went, Early would follow. Early had never truly been hers. Mara was on her own. The first time she'd found herself in bed with two members of her security team, Mara had known things would end badly. She'd thought that it would mean future embarrassment when they sold the story to the tabloids. Mara could've never foreseen this—a hole in her chest nothing could fill.

CHAPTER TWO

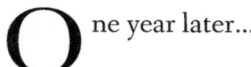ne year later...

"YOU'RE A FUCKED-UP MESS."

"Thanks for that," Mara said, sounding dry even to her ears.

Farrah tossed her dark hair over one shoulder and straightened the lapels of her ultra-expensive business suit. "I meant that with love, of course."

"Of course." Mara's dry tone wouldn't abate. In truth, Farrah had been her agent for fifteen years and had been a rock. Mara knew she didn't mean to be insulting. She was simply honest to a fault. Too few agents were.

Farrah opened her briefcase and pulled out a stack of papers. "As much as I'd love to claim I'm an amazing friend who stopped by for tea, I'm here on business."

"You're an amazing friend, nonetheless," Mara assured her, hoping to make up for her earlier snide tone.

Farrah flashed her a quick smile. "You're too good of an

actress for me to tell if you're lying, so I'll take it. Anyhow," she said, moving on, "I know you're taking things slow right now, while you decide if you're breaking my heart and retiring, but the studio has some stipulations you'll need to meet before Monday."

Mara moved to the window and looked out. "They always do," she said absently, not really listening. It was pretty today. When was the last time she'd gone anywhere? Her home was three floors of everything a person could dream of having. Between an outdoor pool, indoor pool, game room, entertainment room, bar, gym, and everything in between, she didn't need to leave the house. Not even for food since she had an assistant for that. Come Monday, she'd have no other choice than to step through the door and take on the world again. She didn't want it. A hundred times she'd wondered why she'd accepted this role. Maybe because she loved the director. John had always been good to her. Unfortunately, unless she intended to curl up and die, she couldn't hide forever.

"You'll have to have at least one bodyguard with you on-set for insurance purposes. They can't afford to have you sue them because a crazed fan got to you."

Mara couldn't breathe. She kept her gaze locked on the view outside her window to keep Farrah from seeing her panic. Mara hadn't hired anyone else since losing Early and Landon. She didn't have the heart. Now, Farrah was telling her she didn't have a choice. "What will it take to back out of the contract?"

"Are you insane?" No doubt, if Mara had any neighbors within shouting distance, Farrah's screech would've had them calling the police. "You can't back out of a contract two days before they're set to start filming. You'd be ruined."

Mara spent a moment wondering if she cared before

deciding she couldn't be that big of a bitch. That didn't mean she wasn't angry with Farrah, though. "I notice you waited until two days before filming begins to tell me about this stipulation. So, really, who's to blame?"

Farrah held her silence, forcing Mara to face her. Once the ruthless agent had Mara's attention, she finally responded. "You're right. I knew before you signed you'd have to hire a new security team, and I purposely didn't tell you until it was too late to back out. It's time for you to move on."

Mara faced the window again, hoping to hide her anger. Grief had no expiration date. Fuck Farrah for saying such a thing. Mara should've gotten to choose when or if she was ready. "I'll find someone," Mara said, because she needed Farrah to leave before she snapped. She'd find someone, because she was a professional. That didn't mean she was moving on. Sometimes, Mara wondered if she'd ever move on.

BEFORE HENLEY, Kieran hadn't once come in pants. Since marrying the sexy hockey player, Henley seemed to take perverse pleasure in teasing Kieran into completion without permission. The way Henley kept opening his mouth over Kieran's hardened cock through his pants, nuzzling him, left no doubt his husband fully intended to push him over the edge in public today. Public might be a stretch. They had one witness. Cal sat quietly in the corner, nude—as ordered. Pre-cum dripped from the man's erection, rolling down his length. Raised welts marred Henley's back. Kieran couldn't stop smoothing his hands over the marks as a shirtless Henley knelt between his knees, doing his best to blow Kieran in his clothes. Cal wouldn't be allowed to participate. Kieran knew the man wouldn't even if permission was given, but Kieran didn't share. Henley was his, and Kieran would rather die than touch anyone else. That didn't mean they couldn't indulge their darker sides together. Henley liked to be punished. Kieran loved indulging him. Cal... he had his own needs, as everyone did.

The Rabbit Warren was an exclusive fetish club. Everyone under its roof had their kinks. Cal was a good guy. He never touched anyone, and no one was allowed to touch him. This was a safe place. The guy simply watched and obeyed.

Kieran stared down the line of his body at the erection bulging in his pants and Henley's lips skimming it. He'd been acting strange lately. Not discontent exactly. More like he needed something from Kieran he wasn't getting. It hurt Kieran's chest. Kieran could ignore his aching cock, but not his heart. His fingers found Henley's hair and held on. With a tug, he had Henley's gaze meeting his. Before Kieran found the words to dig for the answers he needed, his cellphone rang. A growl escaped as he released Henley and dug out his phone. His work calls were on hold. He couldn't risk it being an emergency.

"Kieran Steele." Even to his ears, Kieran sounded aroused and angry.

"Am I calling at a bad time?"

"Mara? Is everything okay?" It wasn't like Mara to call him on a whim. Not to mention, she hadn't spoken to anyone in almost a year.

She cleared her throat. It was an uncomfortable sound. "Sorry to call for a favor when it's been so long since we last talked."

"Think nothing of it," he reassured. "What do you need?"

Henley popped the button on Kieran's pants. Kieran's gaze shot to his. A devilish light entered his husband's eyes.

"I've taken a new role."

"Good for you. It's time," he said, interrupting her. Kieran didn't usually do such things, but Henley was killing him.

"That seems to be the general consensus. I only agreed because it's being shot locally. That's all I have in me right now," Mara said, trailing off for a moment. Kieran got it. If he lost Henley, he'd never get up again. Mara cleared her throat again. "Anyhow, Farrah—you remember her, right?"

Kieran laughed. It turned into a moan he had to quickly smother as Henley slowly slid his zipper down. "Yeah, she's the agent you chose over me."

Mara huffed. "For the thousandth time, you're a sports agent."

"Entertainment is entertainment," Kieran pushed out through clenched teeth as Henley dragged his teeth down the front of Kieran's boxers.

"Whatever," Mara said, obviously oblivious to Kieran's distress. "Farrah is demanding I hire new guards. She said something about the studio's insurance or some shit about liability for my safety. Either way, I don't know what to do." She sounded lost. Kieran was one of the few who understood. He'd met Mara through one of his star contracts—Noah Cote. Secrets bred friendships, and they both had their share. Mara didn't have anything to hide any longer, other than a broken heart. When the whole world knew your face, being shattered was the biggest secret of them all.

Kieran racked his lust-fogged brain. Normally, he was

the best of schemers. Henley's presence between his knees kept him off balance. "Did they say you needed someone full-time, as in living with you?"

Mara hummed, as if thinking things over. "No. I don't believe so."

"Then just get someone to follow you around in public, on set, and that sort of thing. Have them report daily—get their forty hours a week plus overtime."

"As much as I prefer that idea, I still don't want just anyone hanging around. You of all people know why replacing them cuts so deep," Mara added, sounding like it killed her to do so.

Henley stepped up his game, slipping one finger inside Kieran's underwear, and stroking his erection skin on skin. Kieran's hips left the chair. A small gasp came from the corner of the room. Kieran's head whipped around. His gaze collided with an ice-blue stare. He'd been so distracted, he'd almost forgotten Cal's presence. It hit Kieran. He knew what to do. "Hold on a second."

"Okay."

Kieran held the phone away. "I have a job for you."

"Yes, sir," Cal said without question.

"Henley's going to bring you this phone and the woman on the other end will tell you where to report."

Cal's gaze never wavered. "Yes, sir."

Kieran pressed the phone to his ear again. "Mara, I have the perfect person for the job. He's obedient. I'll put him on the phone so you can tell him when and where to report."

"Thank god," Mara breathed. "Thank you for this, Kieran. I didn't know how you could help, but I knew you would."

"Think nothing of it. If roles were reversed, I believe you'd help in any way you could."

Without waiting for her response, Kieran held the phone out to Henley. "Take this to Cal and then get back here."

Kieran watched as Henley crossed the room. His body moved like a predator, always ready to strike. Kieran's mouth watered. Goddamn, he loved Henley. Always had. He'd give the man anything. No matter the cost. After passing the phone off, Henley came back to hover over him. He stared down at Kieran with hunger in his eyes. Kieran had to know.

"Do you need more from me than I'm giving?"

The lust drained from Henley's face. He dropped to his knees between Kieran's again. His gaze never wavered. "You already give me more than anyone else ever could or would. Not to mention, you're the love of my life. Never think that's not enough."

Kieran couldn't let this go. It was too important. "You didn't answer my question. I won't share you with anyone. Not ever, but I will fuck you right now with Cal as a witness if lashes are no longer keeping the demons at bay."

Pain crossed Henley's features. "I don't know what I want," Henley admitted, confirming Kieran's fears. "You've been bringing me to the edge with witnesses for as long as we've been together." The way Henley bit his lip said he was loath to continue before finally spilling the truth. "It's like everyone here must think I don't please you at all."

Rage had Kieran shooting forward in his seat and capturing Henley's lips in a punishing kiss. He had to eat away those words from Henley's tongue—banish the thought from his brain. Anger and hurt swirled in Kieran's gut. He'd burn this building to the ground if he thought a single person inside believed Henley didn't please him. Kieran was dark, twisted, and obsessive. No one except

Henley knew how Kieran had stalked him until he'd won this gorgeous man. The fact that Henley existed pleased Kieran more than eighty percent of the world. His kiss wiped out the other twenty percent.

Kieran's head hit the back of the chair as Henley overwhelmed him. The man's hands were everywhere. Cool air brushed Kieran's erection. Henley tore his mouth away and went down on Kieran. Kieran's hips rose to meet Henley's mouth as his chin dropped to watch the show. Henley's nose brushed Kieran's skin as he swallowed Kieran's dick. Kieran gripped the arms of the chair, holding on for dear life as Henley destroyed his senses. Henley hollowed out his cheeks. Kieran threw his head back and gasped for air. Henley massaged his balls as if trying to coax the cum out before Kieran was ready. He teased Kieran's slit with his tongue. A moan filled the room. Kieran didn't have enough brainpower left to know if it was his. All he could do was hold on and fuck Henley's mouth. Henley was large and powerful. He spent a majority of the year beating up men on the ice. Kieran's husband was aggressive and full-impact. He loved Kieran with the same passion—full-on, no holding back, and with an intensity most people couldn't handle. Kieran wasn't most people. He was dark. His needs were twisted. Henley was fucking perfect—like his mind and body had been molded to fit Kieran's.

A shout clogged Kieran's throat as Henley squeezed his cock and sucked—hard. He mindlessly reached for Henley's hair, pulling with enough force he was surprised he didn't yank it out as he held Henley in place. Kieran fucked the man's throat, ruthlessly pounding and taking his pleasure. Pressure climbed Kieran's dick before exploding into a rush of euphoria. He gasped for air as wave after wave pulsed through him. Henley kept sucking, swallowing, and licking.

Aftershocks rocked him. Once he'd licked Kieran clean,
Henley kissed a path up Kieran's body. Kieran turned his
head, catching sight of Cal. Cum coated the man's stomach.
Kieran wondered if he'd ever touched himself or if he'd
found release by watching alone.

CHAPTER THREE

Moss hung from the trees, darkening the bright day. Cal traveled the winding back road and considered every aspect of his new task. He didn't think there'd be a huge problem with anyone sneaking into Mara King's home. Hell, he hoped he could find the place. It was a smart move on her part, living way the fuck out in no-man's-land on the edge of Jean Lafitte Preserve, surrounded by swamp. Cal wouldn't have to kill anyone dumb enough to come looking for Miss King. The wildlife would.

The three-story house came into view. It was gated. Cal used the security code Mara had given him on the phone to get inside. After following the driveway around to the back, as instructed, Cal parked beside a red Mercedes and headed for the door. Cal rang the bell and waited. He'd never been one to fidget. He didn't today.

When the door opened, Cal had to drop his gaze to focus on the small man who answered. He was probably no more than five-eight. The guy definitely didn't weigh more than one-thirty, a fact he accentuated by wearing a tight button-down shirt and skinny jeans. He also wore the shiniest shoes Cal had ever seen. The guy had dark hair, but that was all Cal could tell since he never looked up from his phone.

"Good. You're on time. I'm Michael, Mara's PA and handler. It's not Mike, Mick, or Mikey. It's Michael. I'm not nice and I don't care if you are. Mara pays me enough to put up with anything. With that said, Mara is awesome and I love her. If you let her get hurt, I know people who can and will break your kneecaps. Head up the stairs and down the hall to the third *open* door on the left. That's where you'll find Mara. Welcome aboard, Mr. Walsh."

With his high-speed welcome speech out of the way, Michael walked away with his eyes still glued to his smartphone.

Cal watched the small hipster walk away. He wasn't insulted, and oddly—as rude as their no-eye-contact introduction had been—Cal didn't feel slighted. More than anything, he hoped he hadn't made a mistake by accepting this job. It was temporary, he reminded himself. Miss King only needed someone to keep her within the legal bounds of her contract. Cal climbed the stairs. He already knew he could survive hell. This was just a slice out of time—as all days were.

At the top of the stairs, Cal counted the open doors as he passed. Not that he needed to. A loud female voice, singing so badly off-key he wondered if it was purposely done, poured out an open doorway. Cal's gaze wouldn't budge from that space as he moved toward the room. Absently, he noted the dark wooden floors were gorgeous and done in such a way they looked older than they were. Otherwise, nothing penetrated his curiosity over the bright singing. His feet crossed the threshold and froze.

He'd known who Mara King was, of course. Everyone

knew her. Cal had been unprepared for the real, unguarded version of her. In a white silk nightgown that barely covered her ass, Mara looked as if she'd just stepped from the shower. Her skin looked wet to the touch and the ends of her hair dripped onto her gown. She looked unprepared for company. He debated what to do. She obviously wasn't ready to receive him.

"Are you on time?" Mara asked without looking his way, as if she'd known he was there all along. "I can't remember what time I told you to be here," she added with a laugh. She glanced up. Her dark eyes sparkled with mischief and kindness. He'd done the right thing by accepting this assignment.

"Yes, ma'am."

"Oh, good. I'm almost ready." She waved him forward. "Come in. It won't take me long. On set, they always make me wear a lot of makeup and I hate the stuff. So you won't have to sit through that." She whipped the nightgown over her head. Cal turned his head before he could see what she wore underneath. Her voice moved farther away and then closer as if she dipped inside the closet and came out again. "Filming doesn't start until Monday, but once it does, we'll be with each other a lot. I thought we'd go to lunch and shopping today. That way, I can adjust to having a shadow again."

Her words confused him. Considering how famous she was, Cal would've expected her to have a whole team. "Whatever you need, ma'am."

"You can call me Mara. I'm dressed now." Cal's gaze moved back her way. A knee-length sundress covered her skin. "Sorry about that," she said with a sardonic smile. "This is my house. When you're always surrounded by people, you eventually lose any sense of modesty. And, honestly, if I ever want to wear clean clothes, I've had to get over it. Plus, this new movie has two love scenes. You'll be seeing me nude quite a bit, but when I'm at home..." Mara shrugged. "You're liable to see anything."

"I'll only see you when you want me to. Just think of me as an inanimate object."

Mara tilted her head and eyed him as if trying to solve a puzzle. "I could never do that." Her smile snapped back into place. "Which brings me back on topic. We're going to lunch."

"Yes, Miss King."

"Mara," she reminded him.

Cal dipped his chin, acknowledging her words. "Will we be taking your car or mine?"

"Mine, of course. I'd never expect you to pay for gas plus wear and tear on your vehicle to entertain me."

It would be the little things like this that would give away his ignorance. Protecting people, he knew. Just not in this exact capacity. She picked up a light pink handbag off the bed and dug around inside before coming out with a set of keys.

Mara watched her hands as she spoke. "The last team I had were full-time employees who lived onsite. I provided them with an SUV. It's only fair I do the same for you." She fought with the key ring, not getting anywhere. The air changed. He could feel her frustration growing.

Cal closed the distance between them and gently pried the keys from her hands. "Show me which one."

Mara pointed out a silver key with a fat rubber piece on one end. It was one of those that was almost impossible to get off a key ring. Mara moved away. Cal thought she swiped at her eyes, but he wasn't quick enough to be certain.

With her back to him, Mara cleared her throat. "It's an Escalade." Her voice broke. Cal's gaze shot to her back. She gathered a few things from the vanity and dropped them in her purse. Cal stared at the mirror. She swiped at her eyes again. This time, he caught it. "I'm sorry it's a few years old, but I hadn't intended to hire anyone else for a while. You were a last-minute addition." Her chin lifted and Cal dropped his gaze to hands before she caught him staring.

"It's fine," he said, keeping his voice low and hoping to soothe her. "The vehicle is unnecessary if you don't wish to part with it. You didn't say anything about it over the phone. So I don't expect it as part of my compensation." The key finally came loose. Her hand covered his, making Cal jump. He hadn't heard her move.

She slipped her set from his hand, leaving the single key behind. "I want you to use it. There's no sense in it sitting in the garage, going to waste. I've kept up its maintenance. Well, not me. Michael. Did you meet Michael?" Mara asked as she tossed her keys in her purse.

"Briefly."

"Good," Mara said, heading for the door. "You'll see a lot of him. He stays with me while I'm on set to keep me on schedule." Cal followed her down the hall with his gaze locked straight ahead. She hadn't given him permission to see her yet. He wouldn't. Mara kept speaking. "I think you'll love him." She glanced over her shoulder. The light hit her eyes in just the right way, making them sparkle. Cal couldn't look away. "Or you won't," she added with a laugh. Cal couldn't recall what they'd been talking about. He didn't want to notice her as a person. She was a job. Cal got the impression she could never be ignored.

"If he looks up from his phone, I'll decide," Cal said, recalling their conversation. Her musical laughter pulled at the corners of his mouth. He didn't give in to the temptation to smile. Mara didn't need a friend. She needed protection.

"I see we'll get along great, Cal. Tell me you like greasy diner food and I will love you forever. No health nuts on my watch."

"Greasy diner food works for me."

Mara flashed another smile his way. "Great. Pick one for lunch, and we'll hope no one recognizes me."

Fantastic. She planned to get him killed.

———————

IF THERE WAS anything worse than losing someone's love and suffering a broken heart, it was having to pretend it never happened. Every day, Mara got up. Sometimes she had lunch with friends. All the while acting as if her life wasn't in shambles. At some point, a question began scratching at her mind—maybe none of it had ever happened. Perhaps every moment Mara spent living for and loving Landon and Early had all been a lie. Every memory she'd held dear—a figment of her imagination. There might've even come a day when Mara could convince herself of those lies, except dreams of them woke her almost every morning. For a moment, before her eyes opened, it was as if they were still there. The loss was fresh every single day. Even without knowing what she'd lost, everyone tiptoed around her, as if expecting she'd lose her shit at any time. They weren't wrong.

Shopping used to be Mara's therapy. On days like today, she still tried—convinced if she left the house and pretended to be normal, one day it would be true. She flipped through the dresses on the rack. Cal was strong and silent at her back, ensuring no one hovered as she shopped.

Lunch had been nice. No one had noticed her. She could tell Cal had been worried over it. But, honestly, people didn't look closely at other people that often. There were too many electronic devices to keep them occupied. Not to mention, most people were self-conscious while eating. They hoped, if they didn't look at anyone, then no one would look at them. Cal had looked. He'd watched everyone, including her, with hawk-like focus. She would've expected being under such an intense microscope to be uncomfortable. Mara found it oddly comforting—like he was the first person to look at her and see her in a long time.

Mara pushed dress after dress down the rack. She didn't need anything. In truth, she also didn't want anything, but she'd lost weight in the past year. It would come back. The pounds always did, but still, it might be nice to have one outfit that didn't swallow her whole. She grabbed two dresses, determined to buy something. Cal had his back to her, eyeing the store like a man ready to pounce should anyone disturb her. Two women were staring, but Mara got the impression they were watching Cal—not her. Cal was tall and broad. Between his ice-blue eyes and the deep scar above his brow, he looked like the sort of bad boy women liked to tame. She worried more over his safety than hers.

Mara pressed her hand to Cal's spine. His already hard muscles stiffened when she touched him as if he fought the urge to jump away. Before she could stop herself, Mara stroked, trying to ease his discomfort. He glanced over his shoulder, looking every bit as hard as he felt.

"Yes, Miss King."

"Would you stand outside the dressing room while I try these on? People like to try snapping pics of me while I'm changing."

His muscles finally relaxed. "Of course, Miss King."

"It's Mara, Cal," she said for the hundredth time today.

"Yes, Miss King."

Mara shook her head and made her way to the dressing room. The second she closed herself inside, the memory slammed into her, stealing her breath.

With two dresses in hand, Mara headed for the dressing room. She glanced over her shoulder at her best friend, Chase. "Would you stand guard at the door for me? I haven't tried on clothes without security since Early left me."

Chase swiped his dark hair out his eyes. His boyish smile made an appearance. "Absolutely."

As if saying Early's name conjured her from thin air, Mara turned as Early stepped into her path. For a full minute, Mara couldn't do anything but stare at the blonde curls and blue eyes that had owned her for two years. She hurt—all the way to her bones. Oddly, it was a numb throb.

"How did you know where to find me?"

Early's lips twisted into a wicked smirk. "It was easy. I stalk the fuck out of you."

Mara dropped her gaze. She hoped she was quick enough to hide her smile. She didn't lift her chin again until she'd beat her features into being emotionless. "What I meant to say was—I thought you were in LA. Why are you here?"

"We haven't officially moved yet. And, I'm here because you're here."

A flash of pain hit Mara before she hardened herself against it. They hadn't officially moved yet. Fuck her. "You should get out of here before any rumors start. I wouldn't want to accidentally destroy your reputation."

A smile tugged at Early's lips. "I deserved that one, but, baby, I'm not Landon. No one knows who I am. I don't have a reputation to destroy. Not to mention, I don't give a fuck what anyone thinks." Before Mara could guess at her intentions, Early moved closer and touched Mara's arm. "I can touch you like this. We can both smile. Everyone will look at us and not blink an eye because women touch each other all the time."

"You have a lot of fucking nerve showing up here, Early," Chase spat, not bothering to pull back his claws. He knew Mara better than anyone. He understood how much this encounter hurt.

Early's gaze shot to hers. She looked sad. Mara shouldn't care. She touched Chase's shoulder. "It's okay, Chase. I have a few things I need to get off my chest." He didn't soften, but he stepped aside. Mara met Early's stare. "I need to try these on. This one has a zipper in the back," she pointed out, holding up one of the dresses. "Do you mind helping me?"

Early gave a sharp nod.

Mara met Chase's gaze as she passed. "Would you please still guard the door?"

"You got it," Chase agreed, even as he eyed Early with malice. "Someone has to take care of you."

Mara winked at him as a way of thanks as she pulled the door closed, shutting herself inside with Early. She wished like hell she felt as light as she pretended. The moment they were out of sight and no longer in fear of being overheard, Mara turned on Early. "What the hell are you doing here?"

Early's wary expression said she hadn't been expecting Mara's anger. "This is a public place."

"You know what I mean," Mara snapped, uncaring of Early's feelings. After all, it wasn't as if Early had given two shits about Mara's feelings when she'd left.

Instead of answering, Early motioned toward the clothes Mara carried inside. "I thought you needed my help."

Mara kicked out of her heels and pulled her shirt up and over her head. "I don't need anything from you." Her

movements were angry as she pulled one of the dresses off the
hanger and worked it over her head. Mara turned toward the
mirror and eyed her reflection. She looked every bit as
devastated as she was. Her face was pale and her eyes looked
dead. Early's arms encircled her waist before her hand
landed between Mara's breasts, covering her heart. Mara's
gaze immediately dropped to Early's hand. A wedding band
encircled her third finger. The world crashed around Mara.
Every time she thought she had nothing left to lose, life found
a way to strip something else from her. To her horror, the first
tear fell. "You married him."

Early immediately dropped her hand and stepped back.
Mara turned and held her gaze. She had to see the betrayal in
Early's eyes. "Over a year ago, while you were in France."

Mara wished her dead in that moment. Hatred built like
never before. She felt used and insignificant. Unloved.

"Things haven't been the same without you," Early said,
sounding as dead as Mara felt. "There's been this huge hole
living inside me. I go to bed each night without your heat
between us and wake up without you. It's worse than dying."

Hyperventilation loomed on the horizon. Mara slashed
her hand through the air. She couldn't take another second.
The tears flowed without any chance of stopping. Mara
didn't try wiping them away. Early should see the ugly mess
she'd left behind. Mara tried speaking through her tears. Her
words came out in rapid gasps. "You left me. If you're
missing anything, that's on you. When Landon said he was
gone, I knew you'd go with him. Part of me clung to hope, but
I knew in my heart you wouldn't choose me. I was right. As
much as I hate you for that, I'm also resigned. I've always
known I was an afterthought."

"Don't say that."

Early's harsh whisper couldn't stop the flood of

confessions. They flowed as freely as Mara's tears. "Why? It's true. I knew the two of you were sleeping together before you invited me in, but that's all I ever was to either of you—a guest. Hell, an intruder. It was always only a matter of time before you dropped me on my ass." The more she said, the stronger Mara felt. It had all been building and growing inside her since the day they walked away. Before now, her pain and fury had no outlet. Early was here now, demanding Mara let her have it, and Mara obliged. "Maybe that's why I clung so hard and gave so much. I think half the time I was bribing you to stay where you didn't want to be. Landon was easy. He wanted to be famous, so I gave it to him. But you, do you think I never caught the hatred in your eyes when you didn't know I was watching?"

Early took a step forward, forcing Mara to take one back. She slapped her hand against the wall beside Mara's head. With her palm flattened there, bracing her weight, Early leaned in, going nose to nose with Mara. "You've had your say. Now you'll hear mine. I just bet you did see some fucking hatred if you looked close enough." Early tapped her chest. "Because I fucking loved you. Me. But I knew I'd never have you to myself. Landon would always be right there between us." Early's shoulders fell. Mara watched the anger drain from Early's features through a haze of shock. No one could see her face, hear her words, and call Early a liar. Mara needed to know. She hung on every word. Early took a step back, giving Mara some space and making her realize she held Early's t-shirt in a tight grip. Early didn't force her to give up the material. "The truth is, I'm weak, Mara. Landon has always been the strong one. His presence gave me access to you, and I took that opening. I did it with a smile and I swore to myself I wouldn't regret a thing because I had you. But I didn't. Not really." Early's every word found new pieces of Mara's already shattered heart and crumbled them. She felt each word like a solid blow to the chest. Her tears were never ending when it came to this woman, it seemed. She'd thought she'd cried herself dry. It seemed she'd been wrong about that too.

Before she knew what she was doing, Mara's thoughts turned to words. "I don't know how a person can cry so much and live, but somehow I do. This is a pointless life without mercy or hope."

"You're even more beautiful when you cry. Which is ridiculous," Early added, sounding as if it had been an afterthought.

An unexpected smile touched Mara's lips. "No one thinks that but you."

Early shrugged. "They say love is blind, so how could I know if it's just me?"

Watching the L word falling from Early's lips gave Mara the strength she needed to release her hold on the woman's shirt. Mara smoothed her fingers down Early's stomach, trying to wipe away the winkles from the material. She swiped at her eyes. There was nothing left to say. Mara felt nothing any longer except drained. She'd loved and loved, knowing the whole time she had more than she'd deserved. It was inevitable life would strip it from her. "I hope life is kind to you." Mara's nose stung as she geared up for her final goodbye. "No one could ever love you as much as I did, but," Mara said with a shrug, "you only have that once, I think." Mara tried for another smile. "Have a good life with your husband, Early Kincaid. If you would've fought for me, I would've given you the world, but I never would've chosen to be in the middle of someone else's marriage." With her head held high, Mara headed for the door, determined to have Chase send Early on her way. Her fingers curled around the *lock and her dress tightened around her body, holding her in place. It took Mara a second to realize Early held on to the material. With a tug, she hauled Mara back against her chest. Her lips brushed Mara's ear. "Idiot. I'm fighting for you now, if you'd open your fucking eyes and notice."*

Having Early's arms around her was like being set on fire. She hurt. The tears came again, draining her will, but they were over. Everything was over.

———

A SOUND COMING from the other side of the dressing room door had Cal yanking the door open. He thought he had all sides covered, but determined fans could be tricky. Mara sat, wearing the dress she'd gone in to try on, while tears streamed down her face unchecked.

She met his gaze. Mara looked on the outside how he felt on the inside. "It's okay for you to see me."

At her quietly spoken words, Cal slipped inside and pulled the door closed behind him. Her gaze skittered away. She was a beautiful mess. Cal leaned back against the door and crossed his arms over his chest—waiting. Kieran had warned him Mara was fragile. Cal was too good at breaking people, so he stayed still.

"Would you take me somewhere?"

"Of course, Miss King."

A watery laugh escaped her. "It's just Mara."

"Yes, ma'am."

Her smile fell. "I think that's worse than Miss King," she said quietly. "Ma'am sounds as if I'm owed respect. I assure you, no one should respect me."

She meant it. It was in her eyes. Mara truly believed she was unworthy. He knew the feeling well. "Maybe I'm not doing it for you." Cal surprised himself with the claim. He never talked back or made confessions. He bit his bottom lip to keep it from happening again.

Mara stood and whipped her dress over her head. She was free with her body. Cal turned his head. He wouldn't take advantage. He only indulged with permission. Her voice muffled from the material. "I'll probably faint if you ever call me by my name."

"Miss King is your name," he pointed out.

"It's not, actually," Mara said, bringing his gaze back to her. She still stood in only her underwear, but she was in the process of pulling the clothes she worn there back on. "That's not the name I was born with. It's the one I took when I started acting. Fuck," Mara cursed as she sat and pulled her shoes on. "I hate that you're seeing me at my worst on your first day."

"I get paid to see nothing."

Another watery laugh filled the small room before turning into a sigh. "Now I have to make the walk of shame out of here with people taking my pic and speculating."

"I won't let anyone see you," Cal promised as he crossed the room and helped her to her feet. She didn't release his hand. He didn't pull away. "I'll understand if you don't want this job."

She was such a beautiful woman. He would try harder not to see her. Instead of acknowledging her words, he worked on the problem of getting her out of there unseen. "Do you have sunglasses?"

Mara nodded. "In my purse."

Cal glanced around and spotted the light-pink handbag. Without waiting for permission, he dug through its contents until he found the designer shades. He set them on her nose. Cal couldn't tear his gaze away from her upturned face. The tip of her nose was red from crying. Even without seeing her eyes, she looked too trusting to be near him. She was a job. He would treat her as such.

"Keep your head down, and I'll keep you safe from prying eyes." He led her toward the door and kept her purse to use as another weapon to shield her from any cameras. His spine didn't relax until he made it to the car. Once he slid behind the wheel, Cal finally breathed an easy breath. Whatever secrets Mara had, she should get to keep them— like everyone else.

"Where did you need me to take you next?"

Mara kept her gaze locked straight ahead. "Cypress Grove Cemetery."

They made the drive in silence, and at the cemetery, Cal stood off to the side, keeping one eye locked on her while giving her privacy. He watched as she traced the names chiseled in stone. She didn't say a word or shed a tear. Rather, she appeared stoic and accepting. Her expression had Cal wanting the tears back. Crying was a release. Acceptance paved a road to bitterness.

When Mara moved away from the vault to sit at a nearby bench, Cal joined her. He could feel her emptiness —like it was a physical thing. It was the first time he was tempted to touch someone else in years. He wanted to hold her hand. Comfort her. Instead, he clasped his hands in his lap and stared straight ahead, lending comfort with his presence.

"Do you have a family?"

"I'm not married," Cal said, giving more of himself to Mara in one answer than he'd given anyone in years.

Mara's deep, sexy chuckle surprised him. He fought the urge to turn his head and watch the sound falling from her lips. "That's not exactly what I meant," Mara said, saving him from himself. "I meant, are your parents still living? Grandparents? Anyone?"

Cal dipped his chin, acknowledging her questions. He went with the bare minimum. "Yes, on the parents, and one grandmother. I also have a younger brother."

From the corner of his eye, he saw Mara nod, and he lost the battle not to look at her. When he turned her way, she motioned toward one end of the vault. "I only ever had a mother." She tilted her head to one side. "Well, I guess that's not entirely true. She ran away to be with her much-older lover when she was fifteen. I was the result. Her family never forgave her, and, of course, her lover moved on. So it was just us. She died two years ago. Cancer," Mara added with a shrug. "Now it's just me. You should visit your family." Mara didn't sound as if she'd delivered a lecture, but rather like she was sending him on an errand.

"They live in Georgia, but I try as often as I can," Cal admitted.

"Good," Mara said, sounding distant. "You don't want to spend as much time here as I do." She glanced his way. "Is it okay if we stay a little longer?"

"We'll stay as long as you like, Miss King. It's peaceful here. I like the quiet."

"Me too," Mara said, turning her face away, and going back to staring at the stone. Cal couldn't stop staring at her face. She chewed her bottom lip, looking broken, and Cal had never felt closer to anyone. It was the first time he could remember not feeling completely alone.

CHAPTER FOUR

S et life was unlike anything Cal had ever imagined. It swung from constant noise to complete silence, depending on the moment. There was always food. He didn't know why everyone there didn't weigh four hundred pounds each. Since he'd shown up with Mara, no one had questioned his presence. No one spoke to him either. Even Michael, who always seemed to be by his side, never said a word directly to Cal. It was like he was an invisible wall. In a way, it was nice. After all, he liked to watch people. Occasionally, Mara would glance his way and smile.

"She's worrying about you," Michael said, appearing out of nowhere.

Cal glanced over. Michael was playing a game on his phone. "I don't know how you'd know."

Michael looked up and smiled. His eyes were green—like the sea and framed by long lashes. He was stunning, especially while smiling. "I'm watching." He immediately went back to playing his game. "It's my job to notice everything, and I do."

A sharp pain sliced through his head, making his

stomach churn. Cal dropped his gaze to the floor, hiding his wince. It had been a long time since he'd experienced a headache this bad. He lived his life in quiet solitude. That seemed to help. Being around so much nonstop busyness for the past three weeks fucked with the pain management routine Cal had set for himself.

When the nausea passed, Cal lifted his chin. Mara was headed his way and Michael was gone again. The way Mara's brow furrowed had Cal searching the room with his gaze, trying to decide who he needed to kill for upsetting her.

"It'll take them a while to rearrange the set," Mara said without preamble. That wasn't news. It always took them a while to work on the set. In fact, out of the seventeen hours a day they spent working, most of it was spent sitting around waiting on set changes. "Let's go to my trailer. Your head is hurting."

Cal followed on Mara's heels, wondering how she'd known. He always did his best to hide his aches and pains from her. When they reached the trailer, she opened the door for him before he could get to it. She waved him in ahead of her. Cal always wanted to laugh when she mentioned her trailer. Of course, that was what it was, but it wasn't anything like the image the word created. When he thought about trailers, he pictured rundown parks. Mara's trailer was like a miniature mansion on wheels. Aquarium, flat screen TV taking up one wall, a full kitchen, and a huge bed were only a few of its features. Everything shined like new. Michael let it slip the place cost close to a million. As much as he always tried not to be impressed, he was.

"Sit," Mara demanded, pointing toward the bench at the kitchen table. Cal dutifully sat. She rummaged through the cabinet and then the fridge before coming back with two pain relievers and a bottle of water. "Take these."

Cal took the pills without comment because he didn't understand Mara's mood. He was the one hurting, but she sounded pissed off. She moved to stand behind him. He startled when she touched his neck. Cal didn't like to be touched, but he bit back a moan when her fingers dug into his neck at the perfect spot to ease his pain. He closed his eyes. Mara spent a few minutes massaging his neck before moving to his scalp. Her fingers brushed through his hair. There was a real fear he might fall asleep. When Mara finally spoke, she kept her voice pitched low. "If you're hurting, you need to say something. Don't stand there and suffer."

"It's my job to stand there."

A low growl came from the back of Mara's throat. The sound hardened his cock. No one was more surprised than him. Years ago, he'd learned to control his every reaction. He never let himself go for any reason. Control meant sanity. Mara was a wildcard for him. His mind and body never reacted as he commanded when it came to her.

"If you want me to forget you're human, I'm sorry. I can't do that."

Cal didn't understand why she couldn't. He wasn't entirely certain he was still human. "I know you're not like anyone else." Cal heard the words fall from his lips, and they stunned even him. Fuck. What was it about her? She made him lose his goddamn mind. He wasn't star struck. She wasn't the first celebrity he'd ever met.

Mara's fingers dug into his neck once more. "Does everyone else forget you're human?" The humor in her voice said Mara was joking, but she had no idea how close she was to the truth.

Before he could answer, a perfunctory knock sounded on the door, and Michael strolled in. "They ended up only needing to make some minor changes, so they're ready for you."

Mara stroked Cal's hair a final time. "Okay."

Michael leaned back against the door to wait because Cal had come to realize that was what the man did. He silently ensured Mara followed him to where she should be when she should be there. The man never nagged. He didn't have to. There was something about his unobtrusive presence that got people moving.

"Are you feeling any better?" Michael asked, still staring at his phone.

Fuck. It seemed he wasn't hiding anything from anyone. Even the dude who never looked at anyone knew he felt like shit. "I'm fine," Cal lied, because of pride.

Mara snorted as she moved back to the cabinet. This time, she pulled out a heating pad. He watched in silence as she plugged it in and placed it on his neck. "Put your head down," she ordered. "If I need anything, Michael will come get you."

"I'm supposed to be watching you."

"Hush," Mara argued, hearing none of it. She grabbed him a throw pillow from her bed for his head.

"I'll never sleep like this," Cal argued, incapable of giving it up, even as he let her shove the pillow beneath his head and readjust the heating pad.

"I told you to hush," Mara said, heading for the door. "Come find me when you're better and not a second earlier."

Cal gave in and closed his eyes. "Yes, ma'am." Even as he agreed, Cal knew it was a lie. He fully intended to wait five minutes and then go find her. She was his job.

"ARE YOU READY TO GO?"

Cal lifted his head and blinked. "What?"

Mara smiled. She'd already pulled her hair into a ponytail and washed the makeup from her face before waking him. Cal was obviously exhausted. "We're done for the night. Are you ready to head home?" For a moment, Cal stared at her as if she'd lost her mind before looking at his watch. Mara crossed the room and unplugged the heating pad. "It's a good thing these things turn off automatically. You might have ended up burning to death in the past seven hours otherwise. Are you feeling any better?"

Cal stretched and winced. "Define better?" Cal asked as he came to his feet. He stumbled, as if his knee gave out before recovering. His gaze didn't move her way. Still, Mara looked away, hoping to save his pride. The man was the strongest person she'd ever met. She couldn't imagine him ever wanting anyone to see him weak. "Um, just let me hit the bathroom real quick and I'll drive you home."

"Sure thing," Mara said, kicking off her heels and exchanging them for running shoes.

Cal closed himself inside the small bathroom. Mara sat at the table, patiently waiting. She could hear water splashing on the other side. Sometimes, Cal seemed... damaged. Mara couldn't think of another way to describe the way he closed himself away. She had questions she didn't know how to ask. The bathroom door opened, and Cal stepped out, looking a hair better than he had going in. He'd obviously smoothed his dark hair back with water, and his light-blue eyes didn't flash with pain as they'd done earlier. She'd honestly believed he'd drop before they made it back to the trailer earlier. Mara was relieved.

"Do you think you'll live?"

Cal flashed Mara a smile at her question. "Nothing has killed me yet."

His statement did nothing to kill her curiosity. "Do you have a lot of experience with things trying to kill you?"

"You'd be surprised," Cal said before quickly changing the topic. "How was the rest of the shoot?" he asked as he pulled her to her feet.

"Productive."

Cal held on to Mara. She couldn't pull away. Oddly, she didn't want to. "I'm sorry about today. I promise I'll try harder not to fail you in the future."

"Do you ever stop being hard on yourself? You didn't let me down in any way. You've been amazing."

The fact that he still held her hands seemed to penetrate his focus. Cal quickly dropped them and stepped away. "Still, if anything had happened to you, I would've had to live with that. I have too many things to keep me up at night as it is. It won't happen again."

Mara shook her head. "I was working. You weren't really needed. Stop beating yourself up before I start."

Cal's mouth lifted in one corner. "Did you just threaten me?"

As she opened the door, Mara shrugged. "Maybe. I may be small, but I'm fierce."

"Oh, I don't doubt it."

Mara turned, ready to tease Cal some more. A flash of blonde hair caught her eye. The woman was gone, and the moment was over as quickly as it happened, but Mara's heart was still in her throat. Obviously, it wasn't Early. Early was gone. But the memory overcame her without permission.

A flash of blonde curls moving in the opposite direction

caught Mara's attention. Why would Early be skulking about? Mara pushed away from her desk, leaving the script she'd been reading behind. She found Early pouring herself a shot of vodka in the game room.

"Is everything okay?"

Early tipped back the glass, draining its contents before responding. "Of course. I'm off work tonight, and you're busy. So, I thought I might get plastered by myself."

A chuckle escaped Mara. "I'm not working on anything I can't set aside for the night."

Sexy blue eyes remained locked on Mara as Early poured herself another shot and killed it. Mara's blood heated. She wanted everything Early's gaze promised. "Landon isn't here."

"Does he need to be?" Mara asked, taking a step closer, slowly closing the distance between them.

"No. I'm just pointing out the obvious, I guess," Early said before tossing back a third shot. Early swiped her mouth and gave up on the glass. Instead, she turned the bottle up and chugged. Mara might've thought something was wrong, if not for the way Early kept looking at her—like she was about to get fucked on a bar. Early set the bottle aside. Before Mara saw the move coming, Early snagged her waist and spun, pushing Mara's back against the wooden surface and boxing her in. Damn, she always forgot how strong Early was. Early's fingers found the hem of Mara's shirt and dove beneath. She massaged the bare skin at Mara's sides. The way she stared at Mara's mouth had Mara near to panting with desire. "When you were in France last week, everything felt wrong without you."

White hot rage pulled Mara from the memory. She just fucking bet everything felt wrong without her while they were getting married and Mara was fucking clueless. She was so sick of lies. Everyone lied. Everything Mara thought she knew about Landon, Early, and herself—all bullshit. She wanted honesty in her life, even if it hurt. Even if it was someone telling her to mind her goddamn business or to go fuck herself. At least it would come from a place of truth.

She glanced Cal's way.

He tried rubbing his knee on the sly.

Mara broke. "If I asked you a question, would you tell me the truth?"

Cal shrugged but didn't look her way as he unlocked the passenger side door to the SUV and let her in. "I suppose."

She gave him a sharp nod but didn't spring until he was behind the wheel. The moment he was seated, she turned in her seat. "What's wrong with you?"

To her surprise, when Cal turned his head, he wore a huge grin. "That's a long list."

Mara swallowed, refusing to let herself get distracted by the sexy way his ice-blue eyes flashed with silent laughter. She waved off his claim. "Hit me with the highlights. Why are you in so much pain all the time but trying to hide it?" Cal sat back, looking thoughtful. She wondered if he was trying to think of a lie. "Never mind," she grumbled, turning away and focusing on the windshield while seeing nothing. "If you're just going to make some shit up, I'd rather not hear it."

Cal brushed the tip of his finger across the top of her hand, startling her and pulling her attention back his way. His heart was in her eyes. "I'm not one for making up stories, but I'm also not one for soul baring. The short version is, I was in the military and got caught up in some stuff. I saw some horrible shit. Came home a fucked-up mess. Sometimes, my eyesight falters. I have debilitating migraines. This leg is fake," he said, knocking on his left leg below the knee. "It's not a big deal to anyone other than me, so I keep it to myself. Plus," he said with a self-deprecating smile, "no one really wants what's inside this head."

Mara didn't know if that was true. Every day, she found she craved his thoughts more and more.

"Do you need to go to the cemetery before I take you home?"

Without warning, at Cal's question, Mara's eyes filled with tears. "How did you know?"

"I saw it in your face a few minutes ago."

Mara swallowed past the lump growing in her throat. "Sorry. Sometimes, I see things that aren't there."

Cal turned the keys in the ignition. "Just sometimes? That's every day for me." Despite the laughter in Cal's voice, Mara got the impression he wasn't joking.

"Aren't we a pair?"

"Truer words have never been spoken," Cal said, pulling from the lot. Silence fell between them, and Mara tried clearing her mind. Cal had given her a glimpse into his mind. He hadn't shown her anything she couldn't handle. Still, Mara mulled over his confessions for a full ten minutes. She wished she could help. After all, there was nothing she could do for herself. The cemetery came into view, and the familiar weight of her loss landed on her chest. It never got lighter. Nor did she get stronger. Wasn't one of those things supposed to happen?

Cal opened her door and followed on Mara's heels. When she reached her family's vault, he gave her space, but she could still feel his silent strength at her back. Mara traced the letters carved into cold stone. There wasn't enough self-torment to soothe her. Once she'd touched the only thing she had left of Landon and Early, Mara retreated to a nearby bench where she could see their names.

Cal sat down beside her. "Early and Landon Kincaid. I'm guessing, since you said your mother was your only family, that they're friends of yours."

Mara nodded, trying hard not to cry. She was so damn tired of tears. "They were my security team before you."

From the corner of her eye, she saw Cal nod. "I could see you hiring a husband and wife team."

A smile tugged at Mara's lips. "They weren't married when I hired them. Have you ever loved anyone?" Mara asked without thought.

"I thought I did once," Cal said, sounding as cold as ever.

Mara couldn't tear her gaze away from their names. The stone etchings were the only thing that made their deaths real. "What happened?" she asked absently.

Cal didn't respond.

His silence made her want to fill it with confessions. Landon and Early were gone. It no longer mattered what anyone knew. Maybe if someone knew, they'd be real to her again. "I hired Early first. She was this tiny thing with blonde curls and big blue eyes. Her looks were deceptive. She also had a black belt and was fearless. I'd had a woman try to take pictures of me in a public restroom. The incident highlighted a huge gap in my security. So I hired a woman who could go everywhere with me."

"Sounds like you made a good move."

Mara nodded, still staring at the tomb. "You'd think. The studio I worked with back then required I have two full-time guards at all times. Early said she knew an out-of-work stuntman who would be perfect as my second guard. I hired him sight unseen. That's how much I trusted her." Mara took a deep breath. There wasn't a clear starting point in her mind. Maybe she'd been in love from the beginning.

When she looked back on her life, she couldn't remember who'd started things. Only who'd ended them. "There were so many heated glances and accidental brushing of skin."

"With Landon or Early?"

Cal's question startled her a bit. She'd nearly forgotten he was there. Cal was strong and steady, but—in her moment of weakness—Mara might've confessed her sins to anyone. "Both," she admitted without an ounce of shame. She'd kissed her pride goodbye long ago. "By six months in, I didn't know who I was any longer. Two years in, I thought I knew exactly what we were. I thought we were these three pieces of the same soul, fitting together and sharing a life." In fact, those were the words she used to describe them to anyone who knew of their relationship. The joke had always been on her, it seemed. "Landon never really liked being just a guard after having spent some time in the limelight. Acting is an addiction. One I understand, so I pulled some strings and got him a small gig on a limited series shot in New Orleans. Immediately, it felt a lot like we were headed in different directions and I hated it." She'd hated herself too, but that was still true.

"He didn't move out. I took it as a sign that he wanted to be there, and I let that nagging feeling go. But there was another thing tickling at the back of my mind, and I couldn't ignore that. I didn't want to hide." Mara finally glanced over and met Cal's gaze. "I stopped caring what the world thinks. That isn't something I thought I'd ever achieve, but I did —for them."

Cal motioned toward the stone wall. "How did they end up here?"

"Because of me," Mara answered. The first tear fell. She turned her face away. "They didn't want to go public about our relationship, and I did, so they left. I was devastated. It was so easy for them to go—like I'd never meant anything." Mara swallowed. More tears came. "A month later, Early showed up at the clothing store we were at a while ago. We hid in the dressing room and talked. She confessed she'd married Landon over a year before they left. It was one blow too many. I was cold. She wanted to speak her piece. I only wanted to speak mine." Mara froze inside. She fought the urge to run at the tomb and bang her fists against it at the unfairness of life. Most of all, she wanted to go inside and lie down beside them where she belonged. The tears wouldn't stop. It made no sense for one person to hurt so much and live.

"Early looked shattered when she walked away from me. I'm ashamed to admit, I got a small sense of satisfaction in that moment. I wanted her to hurt the way she'd hurt me. She went home, shot Landon in the head, set their house on fire, and sat down to die. I'm stuck here, still on the outside."

CAL COULDN'T STOP STARING at Mara. Everything about this day felt out of his control and wrong. He never stared without permission. Cal definitely never asked questions of anyone. He'd always thought hell would freeze before he offered his opinion without being asked for it. Mara had him stepping over every boundary he'd set for himself. The ones he used to keep himself sane.

"So, that's who I am," Mara said with a shrug. "Are you sure you want to keep working for me? I can fall apart without a moment's notice."

To Cal's horror, his thoughts on the matter took life without his permission. It pissed him off Mara cried. "With all due respect, I've met a hundred people like the ones you just described. I don't think they were ever who you remember them being. That's no reflection on you. I love working for you, and I'm not scared of tears or mental breakdowns."

"Who were they?" Mara asked, ignoring the rest of his statement. "I think you're right about me never knowing." Mara's words came out in a whisper. She held Cal's gaze with her heart in her eyes. Cal knew she waited for someone to confirm the truth she already suspected. Cal gave her the honesty she deserved.

"Early sounds like a woman with no self-esteem who fell in love with a man she felt was out of her league. He had aspirations but no way of making his dreams come true. She would've done anything to keep him happy." Cal couldn't stop. It was like his brain had been hijacked. The cold truth wouldn't stop rolling off his tongue. "Then you came along. Landon saw you running around the house in cute little pjs all moist from the shower."

"Don't say moist."

Cal blew out a breath. "Would you prefer dewy?"

"Not really, no," Mara said, sounding pragmatic.

Cal didn't let it slow him. "Whatever. You looked sexy and lonely. He thought about you more than he should, and he remembered that story Early told him about the time she ate out that girl in college."

"I doubt she ate anyone out in college."

Cal ignored her interruption. "The next thing you know, she thinks it's her idea they lure you to bed. All the while he's hoping that he'll whet your appetite for being with them as well as your pussy once you're all starry-eyed from the dick surprise."

A burst of laughter escaped Mara. The sound didn't soften him. Cal had to say his piece because no one should be as broken as him, especially not someone as beautiful as Mara. People needed lovely things to be lovely for no reason at all other than they just were. "Then, he had what he wanted—a meal ticket, you in his bed, and a step up into the career of his dreams. His wife had you, being more of a partner to her than the man she married. That's who they were. That's why they couldn't have to world looking too closely at it. The question is, who were you in that equation?"

Mara tore her gaze away and focused on the vault. "I'm the fool who got her heart broken." Mara's mouth lifted in one corner in a sardonic smile. "It's odd. When they left, I thought that was the worst thing they could possibly do to me. Then Early proved me wrong, and they ended up here."

Cal stood. Chivalry he hadn't thought he possessed any longer rose inside him. He helped Mara stand, ready to carry out of there. Even once she was on her feet, Cal didn't release her hands. It was the second time in one day he hadn't been able to let her go. Her gaze shot to his. The words came without thought. "You're not a fool, Mara. Those of us who are weak can't stop ourselves from destroying good people in the process of ripping ourselves to shreds. That's not your fault. You're one of the good ones."

Mara's grip tightened on Cal's hands for a second. Her expression screamed curiosity. He wished he hadn't said anything. "Is Cal short for Calvin?"

An unexpected smile exploded across his face. Mara truly was like no other. It was no wonder she was famous and irresistible. "No." Leaving it at that, he picked up her purse. "Are you ready?"

Mara released a heavy sigh. "As ready as I'll ever be, Callum."

Cal couldn't stop smiling. "Nope. Nice try, but you're still wrong."

"Dang," Mara cursed as she headed for the SUV. "I'll figure this out eventually. Mark my words."

Cal kept smiling, because he couldn't seem to stop in Mara's presence, but he hoped like hell she never figured out his name. Right now, he got to pretend he was someone else. Once she knew who he was, he'd still be the fucked-up mess he was every day before they'd met, but she'd know it. He'd only given her the bare bones of his story earlier. With his name, she'd know it all, and he'd become less in her eyes.

CHAPTER FIVE

I f there was a sexier man on the planet than Henley, Kieran would challenge anyone to prove it. He couldn't stop staring at his sexy husband. He knew the man would have to leave soon, and he wouldn't get to kiss every inch of Henley the way he wanted, but still. Kieran couldn't stop staring. A soft knock landed on his office door, making Kieran bite back a groan. He was sick of everyone and their interruptions today. He was still half hard underneath his desk where Henley's friend, Gavin, had broken up their mid-day fun.

"Come," Kieran growled at the door, not bothering to hide his temper.

The small guy who worked for Mara poked his head inside. "Am I disturbing you? Your maid said I'd find you in here."

Kieran bit back his irritation and waved the man inside. "Mike, what brings you by?"

Michael stepped inside the office and held out a bottle of wine with a bow on it. "It's Michael, actually," he said as he crossed the room. "Mara sent me with a gift as a thank you for finding Cal for her." Michael stumbled over the final word as his gaze slid to the side of the room where Henley sat—shirtless and lacing up his shoes.

"Sorry again, Gavin," Henley said, oblivious to the eye fucking he was getting from Michael. Henley's practice partner, Gavin, wasn't as clueless. He eyed Michael with the same intensity, looking as if he'd seen a ghost.

"No problem," Gavin said absently.

Henley shook his head. "It's not like me to be late."

"Did Mara have a message for me, Mike?" Kieran said, snapping his fingers and getting a sick sense of satisfaction from watching Michael cringe at the intentional misuse of his name. Really, though, that was what the man got for eyeballing someone else's husband without permission.

Michael focused on Kieran, looking stunned. "Yeah, sorry. She said thank you for Cal. He's been a treasure and she'll see you tomorrow night at the first game of the season."

"Thank you. I'll see her then. You can go."

Michael's gaze slid Henley's way once more. Henley stood. Finally, he pulled his shirt over his head. His muscles flexed and rolled as he did. Michael didn't look away or move. Kieran set the bottle of wine on the desk with more force than necessary, making Michael jump.

He cast a quick glance Kieran's way. "Have a good day," Michael said before scurrying away.

Gavin headed for the door behind him, speaking over his shoulder as he went. "I'll wait outside for you, Hen, and let you say your goodbyes."

Kieran's ire slipped away the moment they were alone. The way Henley watched him with hunger reminded Kieran of why Henley hadn't been ready to go when Gavin had arrived for their scheduled practice time. The tails of

Kieran's untucked dress shirt hid the wet spot on his pants where Henley had his dick leaking in his underwear. Henley crossed the room. Kieran's cock stirred once more. Henley's mouth covered his the instant the distance disappeared between them. He massaged Kieran's erection through his pants, as if he wasn't leaving.

With unmatched skill, Henley quickly unbuttoned and unzipped Kieran's pants, freeing Kieran's cock. "I can't leave you hanging all day," Henley said as he changed angles and deepened their kiss. He jacked Kieran's dick without mercy. The man knew Kieran too well. He knew exactly how to make Kieran come fast. Even though Kieran didn't have time to savor the building pressure before exploding, he orgasmed hard. It stole his breath and left him gasping.

Henley chuckled against his lips. "Goddamn, baby. That was a good one."

Kieran couldn't speak. He was too busy trying to recover.

Henley glanced down at himself. Cum coated the shirt he'd just donned. "Lucky thing I have another in my bag." He wiped his hand on his shirt as he headed for his bag. Kieran braced his palms on his desk and fought for air as he watched Henley change shirts. His husband wasn't even hard—like their encounter hadn't affected him at all. Kieran's body hummed with joy. His heart hurt. Something was wrong between them. It grew every day and Kieran didn't know what it was or how to fix it. It wasn't even anything obvious. Kieran simply had a bad feeling in his gut —like something wasn't right.

With a fresh shirt covering his gorgeous torso, Henley came back to tend to Kieran. He kept his gaze locked on his hands as he unbuttoned Kieran's shirt. "I love you."

Kieran's eyes burned. "I love you too."

He pushed Kieran's shirt down his arms, undressing him like a child. "When I get home, we'll finish this," Henley said as he used the balled-up material to clean Kieran's skin.

"I'll be here."

At Kieran's claim, Henley met Kieran's gaze. "Am I in danger of that ever not being the case?"

Kieran knew it was true then. Henley felt the same uneasiness too—like the calm before the storm. Kieran snagged Henley's shirt, hauling him forward. "I'm not going anywhere," Kieran swore before touching his lips to Henley's. He wanted to bite the man's lips and stake his claim. Instead, he kissed Henley softly. He needed to know, if he didn't hold on so tightly, if Henley would pull away. Henley shuffled closer, kissing him back every bit as sweetly. Kieran's chest ached. He hated this feeling inside him. Henley meant everything. Without him, nothing in Kieran's life meant a damn thing.

Henley pulled away. He stroked Kieran's jaw. "I love you, baby. Have a good day."

Kieran swallowed past the lump in his throat. "I love you too, and you too. Call me if you need me to bring you anything." It seemed like Henley never remembered to take everything with him to practice.

"I will," Henley said before pressing another quick kiss to Kieran's lips. "Bye, baby," Henley said as he headed for the door.

"Bye," Kieran said too late for Henley to hear it, since he'd already closed Kieran's office door behind him. In truth, he'd been scared to say goodbye. Lately, it felt like every time he did, it might be the last.

SINCE MAKING her confession to Cal over a month ago, Mara had been set free. Having Cal confirm her fears gave her closure. Landon and Early had used her. That stung. Still, she didn't regret them. Even if they weren't who she'd wanted them to be, she'd loved them. She knew that had been real on her end. Mara felt lighter than she had in over a year. Even though singing badly at the top of her lungs and dancing like no one was watching had always been ways she combated depression, Mara loved singing other times as well. If she tried, sometimes she could match a pitch to the original singer; she didn't care that much when she was alone. Acting ridiculous was the whole point.

Mara belted out an old song. She used to dance with her mother to it while they folded clothes on Sunday. It made her smile, remembering those days. Her mom hadn't dated anyone else after Mara's dad left. Instead, she focused every ounce of her attention on Mara. Lilly Carmen had been the greatest mother in the world. Mara missed her like crazy. She didn't feel quite so far away when Mara sang.

"You're beautiful."

A startled cry escaped Mara, and she spun. Cal stood in the doorway, looking guilty. She wondered if it was for sneaking up on her, or for his words. He wasn't one to give his opinion often.

"On the inside," Cal added, looking horrified—like he couldn't understand why he kept talking. "Not that you're not gorgeous on the outside as well, but everyone knows that." Cal shrugged. "You're beautiful on the inside," Cal finished, sounding defeated.

Strangely, it was the nicest thing anyone had ever said to her. Mostly because it was Cal. He didn't speak unnecessarily, so Mara felt like—when he did—he meant his words more than other people.

"You too," Mara said, because she believed it was true, and she knew it would make him smile.

Cal's mouth lifted in one corner, as if he fought his smile. "It would be rude to call you a liar."

"Among other things," Mara agreed. "So," she said, moving on before she made Cal uncomfortable. "New Orleans is playing Phoenix tonight. It's a home game. I have tickets. Would you like to go with me?"

"If you wish, Miss King."

Mara chuckled. "Of course I wish. I'm the one with the tickets. That's not what I asked. Would you like to go with me? As my friend? Not a work thing."

"Yes, ma'am."

Still, she worried he was only placating her and didn't want to go. "Are you sure? It'll be loud."

"It's odd," Cal said, sounding thoughtful. "You always treat me like you've read the manual on my fucked-up brain and know all my weaknesses, but no worries. I can take it."

Mara winked. "I was more worried over your headaches, but if you're sure you can handle it, I'd love to have a friend at my side."

"I can take it," he repeated.

She let it drop. "Second question," Mara said, changing the subject. She held up a black knee-length dress and a similar red one. Mara had been waffling between the two for ten minutes before his arrival. "Black or red?"

Cal barely spared the outfits a glance. "The white."

Mara looked at the dresses she held, wondering if she'd accidentally grabbed the wrong one. She definitely held the red and black. "What?"

Cal motioned toward the open closet door behind Mara. "I like the white shorts thingie."

A smile tugged at the corners of her mouth. She'd asked a man, so she'd had that odd answer coming. When she glanced behind her, Mara spotted a white romper. She snagged it. "This one?"

He gave her a short nod. Cal's body language said he wasn't interested, but something in his gaze said otherwise. He liked the white outfit. She searched her mind, trying to remember if she'd worn it lately. The memory came to her. They'd gone to lunch two weeks earlier, and she'd worn the outfit then. Had anything different happened that day? She couldn't recall anything special.

"Sounds good to me," Mara said, pulling off her robe. Cal turned his back on her as always. "Third question. I don't have to be on set for a few more hours. Should we grab breakfast?"

Cal tossed a quick glance over his shoulder, checking to see if she was dressed. She was. He turned. "I've already eaten this morning, but I will keep you safe while you eat."

Mara popped her hands on her hips. For some reason she couldn't explain, keeping track of Cal's well-being was like a second job for her. She needed to know he was taken care of because he wasn't likely to do it on his own. "What did you eat this morning?"

"Grapefruit."

Mara's nose curled against her will. "Is that it?"

He shifted from foot to foot, looking like he'd been called to the carpet. "Coffee."

"Nope," Mara said, wiping away his words with a wave of her hand. "Not good enough. You have to eat more than that. I'll get you some bacon."

Cal shook his head but didn't say anything.

Mara couldn't take it. "What? It's bacon. I didn't offer to buy you a car. You can swallow your manly pride long enough to eat some real food."

"You're already taking me to a hockey game."

"I didn't pay for the tickets," Mara said, feeling the need to confess. "A friend sent them to me. However, if you're feeling inclined, you can pick me up and pay for parking tonight. It'll be like a real date," Mara added without thought. Cal's gaze sharpened. She immediately wished she could take it back. Cal was a bit like a wild animal—too heavy of a hand and she'd scare him away. That was the last thing she wanted. She got the feeling they were a lot alike. They both needed a friend. Unfortunately, as he'd proven by not using her first name, he wasn't as inclined to accept her friendship as she was his. Cal stayed quiet for so long, Mara worried she'd gone too far.

"I'd be more than happy to pay for parking," he said finally.

She released her pent-up breath and smiled. "Good. I'll buy the bacon," she said, feeling triumphant as she zipped up her half boots. When she stood, Mara caught Cal eyeing her, wearing an expression she couldn't describe. "What?" she asked, feeling subconscious over the way his gaze bored into her skin. It was almost as if he was touching her. She wasn't sure she wanted it to stop, and that scared her more than anything.

Cal shook his head. "Are you ready to go?"

Without thought, she reached for the crook of his arm, holding on to him as she headed for the door. He didn't pull away. His heat seeped into her side. Mara's lips tingled. She almost missed a step as she realized she wanted to be close to him for another reason. Mara wanted to know what it would be like to be kissed by someone like him—dark and rough. At some point, in the past few months of spending almost every day together, Mara had gotten close to him. Even his "ma'ams" and "Miss Kings" couldn't stop the seed of caring from taking root.

"I'm always ready to spend the day with you," Mara said, calculating each word. Making Cal smile was everything, and Mara was just getting started.

HE COULDN'T AVOID SEEING her today. Just as he'd been unable to escape staring at Mara the last time she'd worn the white outfit. The color suited her. It made everything else about her stand out. Her red hair seemed deeper in coloration. Cal didn't know why he tortured himself by suggesting she wear this particular outfit. The one that made her already long legs seem longer, and her eyes brighter. Goddamn, he'd never fantasized about anyone the way he did her.

"Do you mind sitting uncomfortably close to me?"

Mara's question snapped Cal from the daydream of stroking her. "No, ma'am. Just tell me where you need me."

Mara motioned to the empty chair on her left. "Here." Cal immediately switched sides of the table, leaving his bacon behind. Mara snagged his plate and set it front of him, silently urging him to eat. As soon as he was settled, she leaned closer and dropped her voice to a whisper. "There's a reporter to your left, taking pictures of me."

Cal's muscles tensed. He would snap the man's neck.

Mara squeezed his knee beneath the table. A musical laugh filled the air. "There's nothing you can do other than block his view of me."

Cal shifted closer and turned in his chair, making

himself as big as possible, so Mara could eat in peace. Well, as much peace as she could, considering his chest was in her face. Mara didn't stop laughing. It was ridiculous how much that tiny detail had him enjoying himself.

"Eat your bacon."

At her order, he stuffed a piece in his mouth and dropped his chin in an exaggerated motion so she could see he was eating. Unfortunately, the move gave him a perfect view down the front of her shirt. Cal tried averting his eyes. He needed to think of something else. All he ever thought about was her. Maybe it was her past that caught him? It sculpted her into something more like him—made him feel less alone. All the things he did to survive separated him from most people. Mara wasn't most people. Her silence penetrated his thoughts. Their gazes met.

The moment he focused on her, Mara smiled. "You have gorgeous eyes."

To Cal's surprise and horror, he blushed. "Thank you, Miss King."

"What were you thinking about a second ago? There was just a hint of a smile on your lips. That's why I have to know."

Cal's mind went blank. He didn't know how to answer. All he knew was—he couldn't lie. Everyone lied to her. He went with a different yet equally embarrassing truth. "I really like this outfit." It was Mara's turn to blush. The sight fascinated him. "Everyone tells you you're beautiful. Why are you acting shy now?"

Mara shrugged. "I'm not acting. You're probably the only person who would never lie to me, so your compliments mean more."

His gaze moved over her face. Cal could see how much his honesty meant to her after all the bullshit she'd swallowed in her life. He could give her more of what she needed. "You're the most beautiful person I've ever met," Cal confessed, because Mara deserved to hear nice things. "That's not me flirting or trying to step out of my place. I genuinely believe you're amazing." Cal had no idea why he'd gone on so much. He could've stopped at telling Mara she was beautiful. The thing was—he worried he'd never stop. Not at compliments or trying to get closer. Not at seeing her or thinking about her. Cal imagined he would go on forever, dreaming they could be more.

I GENUINELY BELIEVE *you're amazing*. Those words kept Mara glued in place. She couldn't move, speak, or look away from Cal's gorgeous lips—where all his sweet words originated. His lips were plump and looked soft. She craved too many things at once. Mara didn't know where to start.

"You can eat your breakfast," Cal said, scattering her thoughts. "I won't let anyone take pictures of you while you do."

"The reporter left a few minutes ago," Mara admitted. "Once he realized he wouldn't get anything else, he was gone."

Cal didn't move away, even though he didn't need to stay as close. Mara's fingers brushed his thigh, reminding her where she'd left her hand. She stroked, fully conscious of the move. Every part of his body was solid muscle. He was hard to the touch. Her hand moved higher. She wanted to know if he was hard everywhere. His fingertips brushed her bare shoulder, reminding her his arm rested across the back of her chair. She wondered if he was aware he stroked her, or if it was an unconscious gesture.

"You shouldn't stare at me the way you are now," Cal said, pulling her from her musings.

"How am I staring at you?"

Cal's gaze flickered down her body. Mara's nipples hardened at the heat in his stare. "Like I can be fixed," he said. Cal's tone didn't match the lust in his gaze. "I can't be fixed."

A smile pulled at the corners of Mara's mouth. "That's not how I was staring at you."

The heat didn't dim in Cal's gaze. "How were you looking at me, then?"

Mara didn't hesitate answering. "Like if you don't eat your bacon soon, I will."

He pushed the plate her way. "That's fine. I had grapefruit," he reminded her.

Mara pulled a face. "Grapefruit isn't food. It's acid that eats away at your stomach lining. You should eat the bacon. The grease will save your stomach from getting ulcers. Also," she said, focusing on his gorgeous eyes. "I was thinking about how damn lucky I am to have met you—unfixable issues and all." Cal looked away and shoved a slice of bacon in his mouth. She smiled. "See? I knew I'd get you to eat."

"I imagine I'll always give you what you want," Cal said around a drink of orange juice.

"A girl can hope," Mara said before shoveling some pancakes in her mouth. God knew something needed to keep her mouth busy. Otherwise, she might tell Cal all her thoughts. No good could come of that.

ON ONE HAND, Mara was thankful it had been a short

day on set. Cal had dropped her back at her house at one, leaving her to get ready for the hockey game. On the other hand, Mara was a nervous wreck by the time Cal made it back to pick her up. She had too much time to think, and that was never a good thing. Mara questioned her every move. Was she making a mistake? Worse yet, was she making all the same mistakes? Then Cal walked through the door, and Mara forgot why she'd been pacing the floor before he arrived. The man wasn't convenient. In fact, he was downright distant, and—she thought—most likely uninterested. But, he was also fucking gorgeous, and he looked at her like no one ever had before. Mara couldn't stop trying to get to know him.

She'd never seen Cal in anything other than dark business suits. Usually, he looked like a sexy secret service agent, baking in the New Orleans sun. Tonight, in jeans and a white long-sleeve t-shirt, Cal looked more like a delicious treat she wanted to lick. Mara was hard pressed to recall ever being so immediately turned on by anyone's appearance alone. She didn't react right away. Mara had never been more scared of opening her mouth and hearing her lust pour out.

He looked uncomfortable.

That loosened her tongue. "There's a human beneath the stuffy business suits."

"No, ma'am. There's not," he said, sounding one hundred percent honest. His gaze moved down her body, making her want to tug at the tight shirt she wore, and make sure her jeans were zipped. "I can never decide which side of you I like best. I'm leaning toward this casual one tonight."

He gave the oddest compliments. Hell, sometimes, Mara wasn't entirely sure he was praising her. Still, she was always moved. Her cheeks heated. It was out of her control. "For the most part, I'm always casual."

Cal's mouth turned up in one corner. Mara's mouth went dry. "Exactly. I guess if we want a decent parking space, we should go."

"We should," she agreed before she said something she couldn't take back. Like how there was no way they'd been thrown together by coincidence. Neither of them loved themselves, but they cared about each other. Mara no longer knew where to draw the line with Cal.

MARA WAVED AT A MAN NEARBY. His face lit at the sight of her. Cal was forced to pick up his pace as she rushed across the room. The man immediately stood for her hug. She rocked him as if he was an old friend she hadn't seen in a while. He looked nice. His eyes were kind.

"It's so good to see you here. I wasn't sure you'd come." He pulled away and held Mara's gaze. Concern etched his features and Cal knew. This man knew Mara well enough to know of her loss.

Mara visibly squared her shoulders. "What? Me not come? I wouldn't miss seeing Noah and you while you're in town." She turned slightly and nodded toward Cal. "Troy, this is Cal. He's my friend. Cal, this is Troy. His husband, Noah, is Phoenix's star player."

Troy held out his hand for Cal to shake. "It's nice to meet you, Cal."

Cal eyed the man's outstretched hand. "It's nice to meet you as well."

Mara slipped her hand inside Troy's, making an awkward moment seem less so. "Sorry. I should've warned you that Cal doesn't like to be touched," Mara said, steering Troy back to his seat. "Tell me all about what you've been doing. I see you're not using a cane any longer. Does that mean the prosthetic is going well?"

Even as Troy pulled up his pants leg and gave Mara an update on his prosthetic, Cal couldn't tear his gaze away from Mara. She'd never given any indication she knew he didn't like to be touched. The woman touched him all the time without permission. Yet, the first time a stranger had tried to touch him, she'd intervened. Mara was a constant puzzle to him. She made him wish he could read minds. Cal was certain she knew everything and chose to keep it to herself. She intrigued him.

Cal sat next to Mara as she chatted happily with Troy. He chose not to focus on her words. Instead, he basked in the cadence of her voice—the excitement underlying her every word. She didn't smile often and mean it. Tonight was different. Cal was glad he'd come. Someone squeezed his shoulder, and Cal turned his head.

Cold gray eyes met his. "Cal, it's good to see you here."

"You as well, Mr. Steele," Cal said, returning Kieran's greeting.

Mara squealed, nearly bursting his eardrums as she flew to her feet and hugged Kieran. "Kieran."

Kieran smiled as he squeezed Mara. Cal was fascinated by the sight. Usually, Kieran was hard. Stone-faced. It seemed Mara brought out smiles wherever she went.

"You know we live in the same town and you could come see Henley and me anytime you like."

Mara nodded and reclaimed her seat. "I know, but you're both busy men and I've been..." She shrugged.

"You'll do better in the future," Kieran said, as if it was an order. Mara nodded. The crowd erupted into cheers and buzzers sounded, pulling Mara's attention toward the ice. Kieran leaned over Cal's shoulder and spoke close to Cal's ear. "You know you're allowed to bring a guest with you to The Rabbit Warren with your membership."

"Yes, sir."

He nodded toward Mara. "You should bring Mara sometime." Mara turned her head, meeting Cal's gaze, as if she knew they were discussing her. "I think it would do her some good," Kieran added.

"Yes, sir."

Mara flashed them a smile, and Kieran straightened away. He squeezed Cal's shoulder once more before moving along to shake hands with Troy. It seemed the man knew everyone. Cal eyed Mara. Would she go if he asked?

"It just occurred to me, I've never asked how you know Kieran."

Cal didn't know how to respond.

Troy interrupted, saving him. "Who are you cheering for, Mara? Kieran and I have a bet going. He says you'll cheer for Henley."

Mara laughed and bumped him with her shoulder. "You know I can't cheer for either of your men. That would be disloyal."

"Ha," Troy cried, holding out his hand. Kieran grumbled as he handed over what looked to be a twenty. "I told him you'd refuse to take sides."

Mara leaned Cal's way and lowered her voice. "Of course I'm cheering for Noah."

Cal shook his head. "Disloyal to your hometown. I'm cheering for Henley. He has stamina."

"Care to wager?"

The mischievous glint in Mara's eyes held him captivated. "Go on."

She somehow managed to move even closer until nothing separated them. "If I win, you have to stay for a drink when you drop me off."

"Only water. I'm driving," Cal said, agreeing to her terms. "If I win, you have to take Michael's phone away for twenty-four hours so we can have a second wager on whether he'll survive it."

"That's the meanest thing I've heard in a long time," Mara said, shoulder bumping him as she'd done Troy. "I like it. You're on." As if their bet fed her interest in the game, Mara focused on the ice. Cal couldn't look away from her. When she was happy, as she was now, there wasn't a more beautiful person on the planet. He didn't understand how anyone had lived with her day after day, seeing her like this, and thrown it away. What a charmed life her lovers must've lived to be so reckless. For someone like him, someone who'd seen how ugly and dark the world could be, Mara was like sitting in the sunshine. Without thought, his hand lifted. He couldn't stop himself from rubbing one of her curls between his fingers. Mara turned her head. Guilt had him dropping her hair.

She smiled. "What was that?"

Cal shrugged. "I had to know if it felt as red as it is."

Her musical laughter made his confession worthwhile. "Does red have a texture?"

"All colors do."

Mara shook her head, as if she didn't know what to make of him. "You're a strange man." Before he had time to be insulted, Mara linked her fingers through his and all his thoughts died. "I like it, though," she added. "You keep me on my toes. I never know what you'll say next." She went back to watching the game, as if her every word didn't mean the world to him.

Cal couldn't concentrate on anything other than Mara holding his hand. Sometimes he wondered if she even noticed when she touched him. He noticed. Every single time, she had his attention. Cal stared at her profile while she watched the game. He didn't care who won their bet. It seemed she did. He wondered if the way she chewed her bottom lip meant she worried she'd lose, and he wouldn't come in for a drink. Damn, she made him overthink every brush of skin and daring word.

"Mara."

Her head whipped around. "That's the first time you've ever used my name. Huh?" she grunted, sounding confused.

"What was that huh about?"

She flashed him a smile. "I've never thought of my name as sexy. It sounded that way, coming from you." She went back to watching the game. "You're still not getting your hand back, though."

He bit back a chuckle. "What makes you think I wanted that?"

"You tried sweet talking me," she shot back.

"I forgot to tell you something," he admitted. "Earlier, when I picked you up," he added.

She met his stare again. Her dark eyes reflected the light, making his stomach growl. "I'm listening now."

He almost lost his nerve. Cal didn't like to be looked at as closely as she was now. But he couldn't leave her hanging. "You look beautiful."

A blush touched her cheeks and she looked away for a second before meeting his gaze again. "You do too." She went back to watching the game before he could think of a response. He didn't think anyone had ever called him beautiful. Hearing it from Mara, a woman who never said what she didn't mean, it left him speechless.

CHAPTER SIX

As Cal sat on Mara's couch, waiting for her to change clothes and bring him a bottle of water, he'd never been more happy to lose a bet. The brown leather couch he sat upon was the softest material he'd ever felt. He wondered if she'd picked it out or if Michael had. His gaze slid to the French doors. The lights inside the pool made the water glimmer blue. Mara's reflection appeared in the glass and Cal turned his head. She'd changed into a soft-looking pink t-shirt and cotton shorts. He fought to keep his feelings from his gaze. She was the most beautiful woman he'd ever seen. It had nothing to do with her appearance, even though she was astounding. Mara's heart was gorgeous.

She handed him a bottle of water. "What do you do when you're not with me?" Mara asked as she claimed the other side of the couch. She turned sideways and gave him her full attention as she waited for him to answer.

"I get up at five thirty each day and go for a run before heading to the gym. At precisely seven thirty—"

Mara laughed and slapped his shoulder, cutting him off.

"No. I'm not asking your daily schedule. What do you for fun when you're not with me?"

Cal thought about Kieran's words. Something rose inside him. He told her the truth. "I have a membership at The Rabbit Warren." He half expected she wouldn't know the place, and he'd be forced to explain.

Instead, Mara calmly nodded. "I didn't expect that answer, but I can see it." A smile exploded across her face. "Can I guess your kink?"

"I don't know, can you?" Cal hadn't meant to sound as if he was flirting. He didn't take it back.

Mara set her wine aside and clapped her hands like a little girl as she shifted onto her knees. She eyed Cal's features, as if taking her task seriously. "I can't see you getting spanked. You don't like to be touched. Although I could see you doing the flogging. Still, I don't think that's it. No way in hell are you wearing a fake horse head with an anal plug horse tail while someone uses you to live out some bestiality fantasy." Cal smiled in spite of himself. That definitely wasn't him, but he'd seen it done. "Hmmm," Mara hummed, getting serious in her inspection. "You're a voyeur," she said at last.

His lips parted in surprise. Not only had she guessed right, but Mara's expression left no room for doubt. She knew she was right. "I am," he admitted, since it was only fair.

She clapped her hands again and settled back down onto her butt. "Ha! I knew it."

A sudden need to know everything about her rose inside Cal. "What do you do when I'm not around?"

"Drink," Mara said without hesitation. "Seriously. Like copious amounts of alcohol. I should probably be dead," she said, as if her life meant nothing. "Oh, I also swim nude while drinking. I like the way the warm water feels on my skin in the moonlight."

"Does it feel different in the moonlight than the sun?"

Mara picked up her wine and took a sip before shrugging. "How should I know? I'm always drunk."

Even though Cal couldn't stop smiling, he still chastised her. "You could drown or someone could scale the fence. It's not safe for you to do that alone."

Mara shrugged again and set her glass aside. "You should go with me, then."

The words popped out without his permission. "You should come to The Rabbit Warren with me instead."

Mara settled deeper into the couch and buried her feet beneath his thigh. They were like ice. The cold seeped through Cal's pants. He automatically rubbed her legs, trying to warm her. She didn't shut him down. Instead, she looked thoughtful. "I've never been to a fetish club. What would I do there?"

Cal took her question seriously. "Are you asking me to choose a service for you?"

Mara nodded. "You're the expert here."

He focused on her, giving her the same inspection she'd given him earlier. "I can't see you getting spanked."

Mara laughed. Her cheeks pinkened, fascinating him. "Oh, I don't know. I've been spanked. It wasn't terrible."

Cal felt his face harden. "No. No one hits you." He tried relaxing his features. The last thing he wanted was to scare Mara. The flush on her cheeks deepened. Cal couldn't look away or stop. "I equally can't see you wielding a crop." Mara curled her nose at the suggestion. His stomach cramped with desire. "Sensual massage," he said, more voicing what he'd like to see than what he thought she'd want.

"That sounds nice. What's that like?"

Cal was so hard all Mara had to do was drop her gaze and she'd know. "You'd strip and stretch out on a massage table. They'd bind your hands to the wall to stop your natural reflex to push away their hands if they touched you in a way you're unaccustomed to. Your body would be coated in oil and pleasured."

Cal had wondered a thousand times how Mara would look turned on. He saw it now. Her hardened nipples showed through her thin shirt. The flush of her skin tempted him to sink his teeth into her flesh just to taste the heat. She licked her lips. "I don't know. It sounds scary having my hands bound by a stranger. Anything could happen to me, and I couldn't defend myself."

"You could tell them to stop if you were uncomfortable, or I could stay with you and keep you safe."

Mara nodded. "I'd feel better if you were there."

Cal was captivated. She held him hostage with some invisible weapon he couldn't see. "Does that mean we're going?"

White teeth sank into pink flesh as Mara chewed on her bottom lip. Cal's gaze locked on the sight. His teeth were jealous. Her bottom lip looked delicious. She gave him a sharp nod. "Let's go before I change my mind."

THE RABBIT WARREN was a large warehouse that looked like a mansion on the inside. The place also resembled its name. There was room after room—some with open doors and some not. Things she'd never seen and couldn't unsee filled every space. People were openly beaten while others served people on their knees. Bare bodies and debauchery met her everywhere she looked. There was a guy on a leash being led around by a much older woman. They both looked pleased with the arrangement. Mara seemed to be the only person looking at anyone else. Every other patron appeared enamored by whatever fantasy they enjoyed. Still, Mara bit back a sigh of relief when Cal led her inside a private room and shut away the world. She wasn't prudish. Not on any level. Mara just needed time to adjust.

Waiting for her was a woman. Mara felt like she should've suspected it would be, but then again, she'd walked into The Rabbit Warren with no idea what she was getting into. Being nude in front of people wasn't a big deal. After all, she'd posed nude for magazines in the past and she had to be unclothed on set sometimes. Mara tried looking at things like that—like a professional. She was an actress. If things got too weird, she could pretend it was just another role. She undressed and allowed the woman to bind her hands without a qualm. The problem was Cal. His gaze never wavered from her face. It was unnatural for one person to possess so much self-control. He was almost rigid. As much as Mara would've liked to lie to herself, she couldn't. She wanted Cal to eat her alive with his gaze, but he didn't. His control only made her want to work harder to grab his attention. She craved seeing him break. Mara imagined, when he gave in to temptation, he was a sight to behold.

The small brown-haired girl in charge of her massage didn't talk. It was a relief. Mara knew herself too well. If the woman spoke, then she'd fall into too-bright nervous chatter when she really wanted to focus on Cal. He pulled a chair near her head. His ice-blue stare held her gaze without wavering. It should've been uncomfortable. Instead, Mara fought not to pant as hot oil hit her skin. The woman's hands smoothed down Mara's body, starting at her chest, moving between her breasts, and ending at her hips. All the erogenous zones were skipped, making her want it even more. She thought about Cal's confession. It didn't surprise her he was a voyeur. He was deep. The type of man who would need his mind stimulated. She remembered the first time he'd seen her half clothed. *I won't see you unless you want me to.* His words floated through her head.

"Cal."

"Yes, ma'am."

"It's okay to see me."

"No, ma'am. Not tonight."

An invisible knife sliced through her heart. The pain showed in her voice. "Why?"

Cal set his elbow on the table and used his palm to prop up his chin. Still, his gaze never wavered from her face. "I can't watch someone else touch you."

The woman touching her may as well have disappeared. All Mara saw was Cal. "Why?" The question came out sounding like a parched whisper—like the embodiment of desperation.

"Because, even though I know you're not—sometimes— you feel like you're mine."

Mara's throat swelled. His admission made her realize how many things she'd screwed up in her life. Cal's one tiny confession cast a huge light on every time she'd turned a blind eye—accepted less than she deserved. Swallowed Landon and Early's lies. As if the universe chose that moment to push her over the edge, the woman touching her stroked along her slit and brushed her clit. Mara felt nothing except the chill of the air on her skin. A tear slipped from the corner of her eye.

"She needs a break," Cal said, taking control and

sending the woman away. She left without question. Of course, Cal's tone left no room for argument. Mara couldn't watch the woman go. She felt like a coward. Why did Cal have to be so strong and steady at a point in her life when she was weak and useless? "Talk to me," Cal demanded, using the same tone with her as he had the woman he'd sent away.

Mara swallowed again, trying to fight back the pain building inside her. Cal made her want to live again, but she was still the same fool, and her heart still ached. Another tear slid from the corner of her eye, falling back into her hair. She hated herself in that moment. "Am I making the same mistakes again?"

Cal brushed the moisture from her face. "No, ma'am. You're not. The way you keep getting up every day, putting your heart on the line, is the greatest show of strength I've ever seen. The rest of us are just white-knuckling our sanity until death brings us relief."

Mara took a deep breath. It stuttered in her chest. She wanted to know his secrets, but she was also scared to know what made him tick. "Cal."

"Yes, ma'am."

"Would you kiss me?"

Cal eyed her, as if assessing her seriousness. Mara couldn't remember ever meaning anything more in her life. He was the definition of strength. She was the embodiment of weakness. He was always there—watching. His gaze weighed heavily on her skin all hours of the day—like a physical brush of his hand. Mara didn't want some stranger's hands on her. She wanted Cal.

"I can't," he said finally. His voice sounded pained. That was the only reason his rejection didn't hurt. Cal fought battles she couldn't see. Feminine pride had her wanting to cry. Here she was—sprawled out nude for his taking if he'd bend enough to look away from her face. Something else kept her from falling into that pit of despair —the heat in Cal's stare. He wanted her. His rejection had nothing to do with her. "Tomorrow, you have to live with yourself. You should never do anything under this roof that'll make you less once you leave it."

"You think kissing you will make me less?"

Cal's gaze was so solemn, she knew whatever he said next would be the god's honest truth. "I think kissing me, while I still work for you, will be the straw that breaks you."

She'd been right. He knew the truth. "I'm cold."

Cal flew to his feet and grabbed a hot towel. He wiped the oil from her skin. A switch flipped in Mara's head. Whereas the massage had done nothing for her, Cal's touch had her grinding her back teeth to keep from begging. His face was hard. He was obviously disconnected from what he was doing. Mara's body didn't care. She ached. With every fiber of her being, she craved. Cal was efficient and thorough. With the oil wiped from her skin, Cal found her clothes and returned to her side. She expected he would untie her. Instead, Cal slipped her panties up her legs, urging her to lift her hips so he could clothe her.

Mara bit her lip to keep from moaning. She'd never experienced anything as intimate. Countless times she'd had men strip her bare. Never once had anyone dressed her. The act fucked with her head. Next came her shorts. Cal slid them up carefully. Mara obeyed his every silent command. He kept his gaze locked on his task as he zipped and buttoned her shorts. Mara was damn near panting as he put on her socks and shoes. Cal moved back to her head. She stared at his face as he worked. There wasn't a hint of emotion in his features, but she'd never been more aroused.

He slid his hands up her forearms, from her elbows to her wrists, touching her unnecessarily to untie her hands. A stuttered breath escaped her, sounding loud. Cal's gaze dropped to hers. He held her stare and her hands as he pulled her into a sitting position. Their gazes never wavered as he massaged her hands, as if ensuring they had proper blood flow after being bound. The heat pouring off him made it impossible for Mara to breathe properly. He could refuse to kiss her or see her, but Cal couldn't hide the desire in his eyes. There was so much tenderness in his touch.

Although he'd untied her hands, Cal still didn't let her dress herself. Mara let it go on. She didn't want his show of affection to stop. He slid her arms through her bra before pulling her close, encircling her in his embrace and re-clasping the material like a pro. When he pulled away, Mara fought the urge to hold on. Instead, she lifted her arms and let Cal work her shirt over her head. With her shirt in place, Cal swiped her hair aside, making sure it wasn't caught beneath her collar. He stood between her knees. Mara was hyper-aware of how far she had to keep her thighs spread to accommodate his large frame. She felt tiny and safe. Cal's hand moved from beneath her hair to her jaw. His gaze dropped to her mouth as his thumb brushed her bottom lip. The fluttering in her stomach damn near had Mara squirming.

Cal's gaze lifted to hers. Her breath caught. His heart was in his eyes, and Mara wanted it. "I won't kiss you, but I'll pretend I did later."

Mara couldn't ask for more. She'd rather be Cal's fantasy than anyone else's reality. What a fucked-up mess she'd become.

KIERAN'S PHONE rang as he set his belt aside, as if whoever waited on the other end of the line had a camera poised on him. His dick leaked in his pants. Henley's harsh breaths filled the air.

When Kieran answered, lust sounded heavily in his voice. "Hello?"

"It's Cal."

Kieran eyed Henley's bare muscular chest. His gut twisted with need. "Hey. Did you get Mara home okay?"

"Yes, sir."

The man's voice was hard and tight. Kieran knew without being told he wasn't in a good place. "How did her first visit to the club go?" He didn't bother explaining how he knew Cal had brought Mara in tonight. He knew everything. Everyone expected it.

"It's hard to say."

Kieran sucked a breath through his teeth. "That good, huh?" His gaze never wavered from Henley. His husband looked ready to spring. Kieran wanted to see it happen. "Henley and I are still at the club, if you need something to keep you grounded."

Cal sucked in an audible breath, as if he fought to keep his shit together. "Thank you. I'll be there in fifteen."

"Cal," Kieran said before the man could hang up on him. "You know you'll have to stop working for her, right? If you want to fix her."

"Yes, sir," Cal said without hesitation, and proving his suspicions correct. "But she doesn't need me to fix her. She needs someone to love her."

"Do you?"

Cal blew out a breath. "Does it matter? I can't be fixed."

A chuckle escaped Kieran before he could stop it from happening. "You're just a little bent. That's nothing Mara can't handle. I'll see you in fifteen," Kieran said, disconnecting the call before Cal could argue. He'd left his husband on his knees and needed to fix that.

Kieran tossed the phone aside. "Cal's on his way."

Henley's eyes looked half crazed, but he still sounded focused. "I heard."

"You let that Mike kid eye you like he wanted to fuck yesterday."

A line appeared between Henley's sexy eyes. "What are you talking about?"

Kieran hated repeating himself almost as much as he hated the jealousy eating away at his stomach. "Mara's assistant. You knew he had lust in his eyes, but still you took your sweet-ass time putting a shirt on."

Henley stood, as if he wouldn't have this conversation from his knees. Anger boiled in the man's gaze. "First off," he said, ticking fingers. "He wasn't looking at me. His hunger was for Gavin. Hell, they spent over ten minutes in the driveway, chatting after I got out there. Secondly, fuck you. How many times have people watched us together in this club? Not once have I given anyone an ounce of my attention. I'm always all about you. Maybe I should walk out that door," Henley said, pointing toward the door to their private room inside The Rabbit Warren. "And give you a reason to look at me the way you are now."

Kieran swiped his tongue over his teeth. He wanted to fly to his feet and tackle Henley, but he didn't budge. "How am I looking at you?"

Henley's face transformed from anger to hurt. The devastation was in his eyes. Kieran took it like a kick to the gut. "Like you don't trust me. All I have is your belief in me. If you stop..." Henley shrugged. His throat worked, as if he swallowed down words he didn't want to say. When Henley spoke again, his voice came out scratchy. "I can't fight you and me too."

Kieran had never felt like a worse husband. Henley was an addict. A recovering one, but it would never leave him, and that was the whole reason they were there. Pain play kept Henley level. Kieran would be as kinky or as tame as Henley needed. They could go home now and never return to this place, and Kieran would be fine. They could take this to the main floor, and Kieran would fuck Henley in front of everyone if he asked. There was no length too far for Kieran when it came to his husband.

Unfortunately, Kieran realized too late, his anger wasn't about Henley or Mike. It was him. It was Henley's speech about not pleasing him with witnesses. He hadn't stopped thinking about Henley's confession since he'd given it. Failing wasn't in his blood, but he felt like he was failing Henley.

Kieran did something he only ever did for Henley. He apologized. "I'm sorry." He stood. "You deserve better from me."

Henley blinked. "Did you just apologize?"

Kieran nodded. "I'm looking for issues that don't exist because I'm scared."

The line between Henley's eyes deepened. "Wait. Did you just say you were sorry and admit to being afraid?"

The space between them disappeared as Kieran nodded. "I'm terrified of failing you. Of not being enough or giving you everything you need. I don't want you to go looking elsewhere for everything I'm lacking."

Without warning, Henley went back onto his knees and wrapped his arms around Kieran's waist. He pressed his face to Kieran's stomach. "No one could replace you. If you wake up tomorrow and decide you don't want me, no one will ever touch me again until death comes for me."

Kieran ran his fingers through Henley's hair, while wishing he hadn't let his mind get the best of him. His only excuse was—he'd loved Henley from the first moment he set eyes on the man, even before the man knew Kieran existed. The idea of being without him killed Kieran. "Cal will be here soon. Is it okay if I ask you something before he gets here?"

Henley lifted his gaze to Kieran's. "Anything."

"I don't want to hurt you anymore tonight. Can I make love to you instead?"

Henley's gaze moved over his face, as if assessing his seriousness. "Don't do this just to make me happy."

Kieran's mouth pulled at the corners. "I love you. Everything is about making you happy, but that's not why I'm doing this. Well, that's not entirely true," Kieran said with a smirk. "I intend to make you very happy, but I want you." He took Henley's hand and led it to the bulge in his pants. Henley moved closer. His nostrils flared, as if barely keeping himself in check. Kieran sucked in a breath at the sight. Henley massaged Kieran's erection.

"Cal will be here any second. If you want to back down and go home to our bed, I'm okay with that."

Kieran unzipped Henley's pants. He'd said everything he needed to say. His heart needed for him to get as close to Henley as possible. He couldn't go on feeling like something was wrong between them. The next time his jealousy got the best of him, Henley might not take it as well as he had tonight. He needed to fix them now. Something this beautiful shouldn't have cracks. Kieran pushed Henley's jeans down his hips, taking the man's underwear down too. He dropped to his knees, stripping Henley bare. His gaze never wavered from Henley's. Kieran's intensity never ebbed. Henley's hard cock looked delicious coated in precum. Kieran licked it. Henley moaned.

"There's never been a husband more loved than you," Kieran swore as he came to his feet. As Henley tore at the front of Kieran's jeans, Kieran found a sample packet of lube among the goodies provided by the club. Once Henley set Kieran's erection free, Kieran ripped the packet open and coated his cock. He tossed the foil package aside and tugged Henley forward. Kieran captured the man's lips as he walked backward. When the back of his legs hit a wooden-backed chair, Kieran sat, leaving Henley no other choice but to straddle his lap. There was nothing sexier than Henley showing off his strength, clinging to the back of chair while easing himself down onto Kieran's waiting dick.

Henley's heated gaze locked onto Kieran's as Kieran pushed his way inside Henley's hot tight ass. Kieran's balls immediately drew up tight. He'd been on edge from the first lash tonight. No one could make him hotter. Kieran's body begged for release. His mind pled for the moment to never stop. Henley rode him. The man's muscles bunched and flexed with every move he made. Kieran couldn't stop touching him or watching him like a hawk. He was mesmerized by the sexy man he'd sworn to share his life with. There was so much love in Kieran's heart when he looked at or thought of the man in his arms, Kieran thought his emotions would explode from his chest sometimes.

Kieran was so close to the edge, he worried he'd come first. He reached between them and palmed Henley's cock. He stroked, keeping time with Henley's motions. Henley's lips parted on a pant. Kieran could barely breathe. Henley's motions sped, and Kieran knew he was close. He pulled out every trick he had to make Henley come as fast as possible.

When hot cum coated his stomach and chest, Kieran cried out as Henley's ass tightened around his cock, nearly crippling him. An orgasm slammed into Kieran without warning. One second he reached for pleasure and the next the air was gone from his lungs. He couldn't see or hear. His eyes fell closed. There was nothing except the sensation of Henley, taking what he wanted. When Kieran opened his eyes, he found Henley staring at him with his heart in his eyes.

"I think I'm done."

Kieran's heart dropped to his stomach. He would rather die than lose Henley. "What?"

"With this place," Henley said, making things slightly better. He stroked Kieran's face. He looked scared, making Kieran want to rip his own heart out and give it to Henley. "When we started coming here, I was fighting a lot of shit. Now the withdrawals are farther apart all the time. For a while now, I've known something wasn't right, and I thought maybe it was this. It's not. The problem is me. I don't want to do this any longer. That's not fair, I know. You married someone different." Henley swallowed, looking like every word he spoke tore at his throat, or he expected Kieran would be done with him after this. "I don't want to share any part of us any longer, Kieran. I'm exhausted with playing hockey, being the recovering addict, and with this place. Can we just go home?"

As Kieran listened to Henley speak, he realized the man said all the words he'd been waiting to hear since they said their vows. The only reason they were here was for Henley's sake. "I thought you'd never ask," Kieran said, never meaning anything more.

CAL'S PHONE rang the second Kieran ended their call. He checked the face. It was Mara. He nearly drove off the road trying to answer as fast as possible.

"Hello?"

"Cal, I think someone's been in my house."

Cal's foot eased off the gas when his brain stuttered to a halt. His mind fired back to life and he whipped a U-turn without bothering to check if the road was clear. The road was always clear. No one drove down this back stretch. "Go back outside. I'm on my way."

"Okay."

"Don't hang up," he ordered.

"I won't." Mara sounded scared. The knowledge fueled his panic, but his training kicked in, and Cal's heart slowed.

"Tell me what happened. I'm almost there."

Mara took a breath. He heard the harsh gasp through the phone. Damn, he hoped she wasn't crying. Cal hated her tears. "I went to the den to take my wine glass to the kitchen. Your empty water bottle was still there, but my glass was gone. So I went to the kitchen, hoping maybe I'd carried it there earlier and forgotten, even though I know that's not the case. I clearly remember draining the glass and leaving it on the table. Anyhow, no glass."

That was fucking odd. "Did Michael come by?"

"No. That was my first thought too," Mara said, dashing his hopes something fucked up wasn't happening. "I called him and he said it wasn't him. So, at this point, I'm still thinking it's no big deal. It's just a missing glass, but then, I went to my bedroom, and one of my dresses was spread out on the bed. In my spot. Like it was me." Mara's voice broke. Cal's foot pressed harder on the gas. The house came into view. His training went out the window. If anything happened to Mara...

"I'm here," he said, tearing into the driveway. He caught sight of Mara standing outside the glass French doors by the garage. As he looked on, she disconnected their call. He jumped from his truck and was headed her way before the phone left his ear. Even in the dark, he could see how pale she was. He didn't hesitate pulling her into his arms and holding her against his chest.

"We need to call the police," he said, speaking against the top of her head. It wasn't until his lips brushed her skin with each syllable that he realized he'd been kissing her head. His heart raced from the fear and other things he didn't want to admit. "They need to dust for prints and have a look at your surveillance cameras."

Mara nodded against his chest. "Okay."

"I'll take care of everything."

"I know."

The trust in her voice was undeniable. She was the only person Cal didn't know how to let down. He could and probably would fail the rest of the world, but never her. Even after the police arrived, Mara never moved from his hold. She answered every question from his arms. No one batted an eye. To the rest of the world, they appeared normal. Cal realized something as he rubbed Mara's back and waited for the police to finish doing their part. Mara had spent the last few months taming him like a wild animal. His revelation came at the worst moment. He tried not to laugh at the train of his thoughts. While she'd been protecting him from other people's touches, she'd been brushing and stroking his skin every chance she could. Now, in her time of need, he couldn't stop holding her, trying to keep her physically safe. Before Cal could find the words to express how she impacted his life, the police officer who'd responded to her call reappeared.

"I'm not sure how to classify this one, Miss King," Officer Davies said after searching the house and checking the surveillance. "Is anything missing other than a wine glass?"

Mara shook her head. "Not that I noticed, but I didn't look too closely. Cal told me to get out and wait for you."

The officer nodded. "That was the smart thing to do." He wrote something on a card and handed it to her. "If you notice anything else missing after I'm gone, call that number and let me know. I'll add it to the police report. Otherwise, I'm not sure what to tell you. There're no signs of forced entry. Your alarm didn't go off, and your cameras didn't catch anything. It seems kind of strange to me. Are you sure you didn't just set the glass down somewhere and forget it?"

Cal felt Mara's muscles tense, as if she fought the urge to snap. "Yes, I'm sure." The way she said the words through clenched teeth spoke volumes about her level of irritation.

Officer Davies scratched his chin. "Well, I could swing by here a couple of extra times tonight to check on you, if you'd like." Even though his tone didn't change, Cal saw a glint in the man's eyes he didn't like.

Cal steered Mara toward the back door. "That won't be necessary. Miss King won't be staying here tonight. Go get what you need for the night," he told Mara, giving her a small push toward the door. He turned his attention toward the cop, ready to send him on his way.

Mara didn't budge. He glanced her way. The way she chewed on her bottom lip ripped at his heart. "Will you come with me?" There was no resisting her plea.

"Yes, ma'am." Even Cal heard the affection in his tone. He focused on the cop once more. "Thank you for your assistance. If anything else is missing, Miss King's assistant, Michael, will send you the list."

The man didn't look happy about his contact being downgraded to an assistant, but he nodded. "I'll keep an eye out. You two have a good night." With a nod, he walked away.

Cal walked Mara inside, keeping one hand pressed to the small of her back. The house had been searched by the police, but Mara was still spooked. He would do whatever she needed. As he watched her pack a bag, and dip in and out of the bathroom, brushing her teeth and washing her face, he couldn't lie to himself. His need to protect her had nothing to do with his job. The way he felt about her extended way beyond that. They were friends, but he wanted more. He'd already admitted as much to her back at the club. Filming was almost at an end. Soon she wouldn't need him any longer. The problem was, he didn't know how to stop needing her. Someone had been in her house tonight, he was sure of it no matter what the police thought. If he'd gone home earlier, rather than inviting her out, he couldn't think about what might've happened to her. Cal couldn't leave her here and go home. She was his responsibility. Not because of a job, but because she was his, even if she never really was. He'd do anything for Mara, even if it meant walking away from this bullshit job so he could be what she really needed.

CHAPTER SEVEN

The bed Kieran shared with Henley had never felt so good. They hadn't wasted any time skipping out of the club once Henley had made his confession. Now, cuddled in the bed they slept in every night, Kieran felt full for the first time in a while. All doubts had been erased by only a few words. He felt like he had his husband back. Kieran never wanted to leave their bed or stop holding Henley ever again.

"It just occurred to me that Cal never showed up and we never called to let him know we were leaving."

Kieran bit his bottom lip at Henley's observation. He was glad it was too dark for Henley to see his guilt. In the end, Henley was the one person Kieran would never lie to. "I knew he wouldn't show."

Henley lifted his head from Kieran's chest. Even in the dark, he could feel Henley's gaze on him, searching for answers. "What did you do?"

Kieran shrugged. "He needed a little push."

"What did you do?" Henley repeated. He didn't sound angry, only certain Kieran had meddled, because Kieran always did. To be fair, Kieran was always right. This was no different.

"He's had a few months with Mara. They should be doing more than holding hands by now, which is all they did at the game tonight."

Henley swiped his hand over his face. "Jesus. How do you know they're not fucking in every corner of her home?"

"First off, he wouldn't have called us tonight if they were. Secondly, I saw his face tonight when she took his hand. He was surprised."

"You know they're both one heartbreak away from never recovering," Henley said, sounding more resigned than angry.

"It was a carefully calculated move. Nothing too horrible. Just enough, that even if they don't end up together, it'll definitely highlight that Mara needs to stop pretending she doesn't need security. For Cal, it'll kick his need to be needed and to protect others into gear. Plus, he needs to be reminded he's strong."

"Shit," Henley groaned, dropping his head back to Kieran's chest. "I don't even want to know the details."

Kieran smiled into the dark as he brushed his fingers through Henley's hair. "That's probably for the best, even though you're my husband and can't be forced to testify against me in court."

Henley's groan was long and loud, making Kieran's smile grow. "I'm convinced—if I didn't keep you busy— you'd take over the world."

"I already have it," Kieran admitted, needing Henley to know he was everything. "When I won you, that was world domination for me."

Henley's lips brushed Kieran's throat. "Funny how that

hasn't stopped you from meddling," he said between placing kisses against Kieran's neck.

"Interfering in other people's lives is just hobby to keep me distracted while you're working. Speaking of which..."

"Let's not talk about it now," Henley begged as he straddled Kieran's hips.

Kieran stared up at him, willing to give him anything. "Whatever you want. I can iron out the details of your retirement first thing in the morning," Kieran added, because he was still in charge and they would talk about this.

Henley's smile said he wasn't bothered. "You just couldn't let that pass. Could you?"

"You should've seen it coming."

"I really should have," Henley admitted, leaning down and touching his lips to Kieran's. Kieran's heart soared. Honestly, it didn't matter what happened tomorrow with Henley's career. Whatever came next, they were in it together.

<hr>

CAL'S HOUSE was a lot nicer than Mara imagined. It wasn't that she'd thought he lived in a dive somewhere. Cal was a single guy. She'd expected a bachelor pad. His house was gorgeous. It wasn't huge. From the quick tour he'd given her, she knew he had four bedrooms, one he used as an office, and another as a home gym. She didn't try staying in the spare, and Cal didn't try making her.

"Would you like something to drink?"

Mara shook her head at Cal's questions. "I think I just want to go to bed. It's been a day."

Cal's expression remained solemn as he nodded. "My room is down here."

Mara followed him down the hall. Even through his t-shirt, she could see the way his muscles moved. Her mouth went dry. Maybe she should've taken that drink after all. There was no chance they'd be doing anything other than sleeping. Cal had made his position clear. He worked for her. That was a line he wouldn't cross. All the knowledge and good sense in the world didn't stop her from wanting to run her palm up his back and feel those muscles that were teasing her. It had been so damn long since she'd really touched anyone. Mara wasn't sure she still had it in her. Maybe she would destroy Cal if she tried. Maybe that was all she ever did.

They were standing inside a military clean room without Mara's brain on board. She'd been too busy enjoying the vision of Cal to really inspect the house. She glanced around the room, giving her eyes something else to do. The bed was a queen—like he didn't share it and never intended to do so. She set her bag in a chair near the bed.

"I need to get ready for bed. If you need this bathroom," Cal said, motioning toward an open doorway inside the bedroom. "I can use the one down the hall."

Mara shook her head. "Go ahead. I'm sure all your stuff is in there. I can find the one down the hall if I need it."

With a nod, Cal headed inside and closed the door between them. While Cal was in the bathroom, Mara undressed and pulled on her gown. The bathroom door opened. Cal stepped out wearing a t-shirt that stretched too tight across his muscles and a pair of pj pants. Mara could barely breathe. Cal put off such a menacing vibe, Mara wasn't sure anyone looked too closely at him. She did. He was beautiful. Cal always flinched when anyone accidentally brushed against him, or walked too close, for that matter. Mara wanted to run her hands all over him and feel him go hard beneath her touch. She somehow managed to fight the temptation.

Instead, she motioned toward a lamp in the corner. "Is it okay if we leave that light on? I don't like the dark."

Cal nodded as he pulled the covers back on the bed without looking at her. "I never turn it off," he said as he sat on the edge of the mattress with his back to her. "Sorry about this." Cal removed his prosthetic and set it aside. "I can't sleep with it on." He still wasn't looking at her. It was making Mara a little nuts.

She climbed onto the bed. "Why are you apologizing? I just admitted to a fear of the dark." She snuggled down beneath the covers. They smelled clean. Crisp—like fresh from the dryer. Mara caught herself snuggling deeper to get a better sniff.

Cal glanced over his shoulder. "There are ghosts in the dark." He wasn't teasing her. Cal meant it. "I never sleep with the light off."

Mara turned on her side, facing him when he finally stretched out beside her. "When Landon and Early died, I started alternating between sleeping with the light on and off. It was an experiment to see which felt emptier. You'd think the dark would hide the emptiness, but it doesn't. It made me forget I was alone, and that's worse than having the light on."

"I have nightmares," Cal said, sounding ashamed. "That's why I'm only staying here until you fall asleep. I don't want to risk accidentally hurting you if I wake up not knowing where I am. Once you're asleep, I'll move to the chair."

Considering his headaches, Mara was horrified by the

thought of him sleeping sitting up. "No. You're staying put. If anyone needs to sleep in the chair, I'll do it."

To her surprise, Cal chuckled. It was low, deep, and oh so fucking hot. "It's not like I don't have another bed. I want to watch over you."

"You're not doing it from the chair," Mara said, digging her heels in. "I swear you won't hurt me."

Cal shook his head, but he was still smiling. "You can't promise that."

Stubbornness Mara hadn't experienced in a long time set in. "I can promise any damn thing I like. You're not sleeping in the chair. If you have a nightmare, I'll take care of you. Understood?"

Laughter danced in Cal's eyes, making him look ten years younger. "Yes, ma'am."

"How old are you?" Even Mara didn't know where the question came from. She simply wanted to know everything about him.

"Thirty-four. It's legal for you to be in bed with me," he added with laughter lacing his words.

Without thought, she punched him in the arm. She half expected he'd transform into the version of himself everyone else saw the moment her fist connected with his arm. Instead, his smile grew and he rubbed the spot where she'd hit him. Her chest warmed. She closed her eyes against the sight of him before she did something stupid. "Smart ass," she grumbled to herself. "I'm thirty-two, by the way," she said when it occurred to her she hadn't given him the same information he'd given her.

"I know," he said quietly, as if trying to soothe her into sleeping. "Before my first day, I researched you." He brushed her hair away from her face. Mara fought the urge to open her eyes and stare at him some more. His fingertips skimmed her jaw. Her nipples hardened. She wanted to crawl across the bed and straddle his body—test his control. But Cal was right; she'd couldn't do those things as long as he worked for her. Landon and Early had scarred her. If she touched him, and he let her, she'd always wonder if he used her for some gain. She'd always worry it was a game. Mara needed someone who didn't depend on her. She wanted someone who wanted her for her and not what she could do for them.

IT HADN'T BEEN Cal's intention to ever touch her. Lusting from afar was more his thing. Mara closed her eyes, leaving Cal free to stare at her without judgment or witnesses. So he did. She looked young, alone, and vulnerable. There was nothing tainted about her despite her beliefs to the contrary. Mara hurt but kept on living—just like him. She was so goddamn beautiful, and she smelled like heaven. An itch started at the back of his brain. Mara was the only person whose touch didn't hurt. A question nagged at his gut. What would happen if he kissed her? He needed to know.

"Mara."

"Yes?" She was sweet and trusting. Her eyes never opened—like she was safe with him. She wasn't.

"I know you still need me to keep you in contract for the final weeks of filming. For that reason, I'll keep going with you to the set, but I quit."

A line appeared between her eyes a half second before they flew open. "What? Why?"

Cal shifted onto his elbow, hovering over her. "It's not personal," he promised. "I'm about to cross a line," he said before covering her mouth with his. Mara didn't push him away or tense. Still, he only pressed his lips to hers and waited. Cal didn't know if he expected a nightmare would claim him and rip him away from the moment or if he thought Mara would hit him, but he couldn't move. He was frozen with his lips clinging to hers. Fear and uncertainty owned him. It had been seven years since he'd kissed anyone. That was a hell of a statistic to pull from his brain at that exact moment. The shaking in his gut could've been fear or lust. He no longer knew.

Mara opened her mouth and sucked his bottom lip between her teeth and tugged. Lust won. His body didn't need his brain's permission any longer. Without thought, he delved inside, licking the edge of Mara's tongue. His weight shifted until Cal found himself cradled between Mara's thighs. As their tongues clashed, Cal's hips moved. His erection ground against her mound. Their clothes irritated his skin. A thin layer of sweat broke out across his body. His fingers found the edge of her gown and pushed it higher. He needed to feel her perfection. She was as unblemished as he was scarred. The more of her he bared, the more Cal wanted. He kept dragging the material higher until Mara let him pull it up and over her head. He tossed it aside and reclaimed her mouth. It might've been seven years, but he hadn't forgotten what he liked. Cal nibbled on Mara's lips as he toyed with her bare breasts. He wanted to taste her. All of her. He shifted lower. His teeth scraped her throat as headed south. The tiny sounds escaping Mara drove him. He needed those whimpers to turn to moans. Cal nipped at her collarbone before moving to her breasts. He took turns lapping at her nipples. His dick leaked in his underwear. He ignored it. By now, his cock should be used to neglect. Mara was the exception to every rule he'd set for himself.

Masturbation meant letting go—feeling. Cal didn't like to feel. Mara had his body on fire. He felt everything, except the pain he expected. Even his thoughts seemed to belong to her. Nothing touched him except her.

Cal's lips kept moving lower. He had to know. He couldn't recall the last time he'd been filled with such an insatiable need to fucking know how every inch of someone tasted. Mara's body had been teasing him for months, no matter how hard he tried not to see her. Mara was all he ever saw. Even when his eyes were closed.

His fingers grasped the edge of her panties as his tongue circled her navel. Her hips lifted, giving him all the permission he needed to slip them down. He shifted onto his knees long enough to slide her underwear off and toss them aside. As much as he wanted to stay in that position, eating her alive with his gaze, Cal's tongue demanded he get back to work. Memorizing the taste of her body was a job that wouldn't do itself. For a half second, before his lips collided with her skin, the flush covering her body fascinated him. She was turned on. It struck him as odd. He'd been so focused on what he wanted, he'd stopped considering her reactions. Cal needed this. He needed her.

Without preamble, he tossed her leg over his shoulder and opened his mouth over her pussy. His eyes fell closed as he tongued her hole and slit. He licked and nipped with no real goal in mind beyond savoring his meal. Mara moved against his mouth. A loud moan filled the room, penetrating his haze. His purpose shifted. He needed her to make that sound again. Cal found her clit and sucked. Mara's fingers found his hair and tugged. A smile curled his lips. He circled the tiny bud with his tongue. She whimpered. He wanted her to scream. Cal flattened his tongue against her clit and lapped at it without mercy. Every sound she made had him craving another, until she writhed beneath him. Her muscles tensed. He doubled his efforts, delving his fingers inside, mimicking the way he'd fuck her. His name left her lips as her channel pulsed around his fingers. Air left his lungs like he'd been running a marathon as he kissed his way back up her body. His stomach shook as their lips met. The inside of his underwear was soaked, but he already knew he wouldn't find relief. He'd gone farther tonight than he had in years. His neck ached and his head pounded from holding back the floodgates. Hot tears pressed at the backs of his eyes, making him feel weak. This woman letting him touch her was beautiful inside and out. He wasn't. Cal was horribly scarred beneath his clothes. Under his skin, he was irreparable.

Mara's tongue brushed his sweetly, accepting her own juices. Damn, everything about her got to him. Her hand slid lower, finding the edge of his pants. He covered her hand with his, stopping her before she delved inside. He dragged her hand higher, bringing it to his lips as he rolled to his side, putting his weight on his hip so he wouldn't squash Mara.

Cal took his time, kissing each knuckle. He kept his eyes pressed tightly closed. If Mara was disappointed in him, he couldn't see it. Everything felt ready to break. "Thank you," he whispered, holding her hand to his mouth. Even if this was the worst sexual encounter of Mara's life, he needed her to know she'd given him more than he'd thought to ever have again. He'd thought any sense of intimacy was lost to him forever. Even if Mara never spoke to him again, once filming ended, he'd think about her for the rest of life.

MARA CAME AWAKE WITH A START. She glanced at the clock. Barely two hours had passed, but she hadn't realized she'd fallen asleep. The bed beside her was empty. Her gaze shot toward the chair. It was empty as well. After finding her gown, she went in search of Cal. She poked her head in each room she passed, barely sparing them a glance each time she didn't find Cal. Finally, she found him working out in the home gym. Her feet froze to the floor at the first sight of him. He wore only shorts. Sweat glistened on his hard body. The power he showed had her sitting on the floor near the door, hoping not to get caught watching. Each pull up Cal did was done with ease—like a machine, perfectly timing each lift. Mara was mesmerized. Cal's body was scarred in a way she couldn't have imagined. Deep lines and ragged marks marred his back. It looked as if chunks had been cut from his flesh and left to heal with no medical treatment. Her heart broke for the pain he must've endured. Her body ached to feel him pressing against her once more. Scars were nothing. Cal was fucking sexy as sin. Strength oozed from his pores, making her long to lick him just to get a taste. She pressed her knees together to ease the building ache.

Cal dropped from the bar and turned. Their gazes collided and he froze. His lips parted in surprise. Mara's gaze slid down his body. His front was every bit as scarred as the back. Those abs, though. Mara's mouth watered. Cal reached for his shirt. Mara moved to her feet and closed the distance between them before Cal could cover himself. She didn't want him to hide. Not from her.

She grabbed his shirt, intent on tossing it away. A slight tug of war ensued before Cal finally let her have it. The wary look in his eyes made her chest hurt. She couldn't let this go on. Uncaring of the sweat coating his skin, Mara invaded his space. Her fingers skimmed his chest, his sides, and his abs.

She kissed the spot between his pecs where a long, jagged scar ran the length of his torso. "I woke up alone," she said against his skin, trying to keep the accusation from her voice.

His fingers found her hair. She felt the lightest brush through her curls. "I couldn't sleep."

"You should've woke me. I would've kept you company." Mara couldn't stop touching him as she made the claim.

"I thought you said no health nuts on your watch," Cal said with laughter lacing his words.

Mara took a step back and looked up at the bar Cal had been using moments earlier. "Who knows. I might not be too bad at this." She jumped, snagging the bar and pulling herself up. A laugh escaped her as her gown rose a little too high and she realized she'd forgotten her panties. Now she had to try to get back down with her dignity intact.

Cal's hands moved up the backs of her thighs as he moved in and urged her legs around his waist. He encircled her hips and she let go, trusting he wouldn't let her fall. Mara automatically wrapped her arms around his neck and held on. Up close, Cal's light blue eyes were even more amazing. Mara couldn't look away.

"I need a shower."

Mara didn't release him. "Are you running away?"

Cal licked his lips, drawing Mara's gaze their way. Damn, she wanted to taste them again, but she had to stop Cal from getting away. He didn't respond to her question. Mara found the curls at his nape and toyed with them, refusing to move from his hold.

"Talk to me, Cal. What's the worst that could happen if you stayed like this just a few moments longer?"

"I could decide I love you a half second before I watch your expression turn to hate when you realize I'm way more fucked up than you believe." Every word Cal spoke punched Mara in the chest. Not because Cal believed they were true, but because Mara wanted him to love her. A sardonic smile touched Cal's lips. "I can see it in your eyes that you know I'm right."

Mara shook her head. "That's not what you're seeing."

"What am I seeing?" Cal asked quietly, as if scared of spooking her.

"Longing." The word barely died on her lips before Cal's mouth met hers. It was an explosion of heat. Cal's tongue filled her mouth. She sucked, needing all of him. His kiss gentled, so did Mara. He led her every move. She let it happen. The way he licked the edge of her tongue was everything. Mara never wanted it to end. She tried touching every inch of him she could reach. Cal did something for her she'd never thought to have again. He kissed her like she mattered.

Cal pulled away. "There isn't a single condom in this house."

Mara shook her head. "That's not what I'm after."

His gaze never wavered from hers. "What are you after?"

"This," Mara admitted. "Just this."

One of Cal's knees hit the floor, followed by the other. He held tightly to her body until he could gently lower her onto her back. The way he held her stare as he covered her body with his had Mara breathless. She hadn't lied. This was all she wanted. She didn't want to push Cal. He needed patience and time. Cal deserved someone with a beautiful soul. Someone who could heal him.

"You deserve someone better than me," Mara said, clinging tightly to Cal despite her claim.

Cal's mouth lifted in one corner. "What would I do with someone untouched by life? They'd never understand me. Not like you do," Cal said before capturing her lips once more. This time, it was different. He was soft. Mara couldn't think any longer. All she could do was feel. She had time later to remind herself of all the ways she could fail him.

CHAPTER EIGHT

Cal's head was pounding. His neck hurt and his eyes burned. To make matters worse, Mara was headed to her trailer for a hair and makeup touch-up with the world's chattiest artist, Candy. The woman never stopped talking. She told everything to anyone who would listen. Unfortunately, the extent of what the woman knew beyond making someone beautiful was the line of men she slept with. Cal didn't care that she obviously slept with everyone. He didn't judge. But his head hurt, and today wasn't the day. It was Mara's last day on set. They needed to talk about where they were headed after this. He needed to be sharp. It wasn't happening.

Mara kept flashing him the side eye, and he kept his features blank. He'd never voiced his dislike of listening to Candy ramble on, but Mara always seemed to know everything about everything when it came to him. He was angry today. Not for anything Mara had done. Cal just hated feeling bad. He'd kept his promise to Mara by continuing to come to the set with her. After the incident at her house, Mara had stayed with him for three nights before returning home. Nothing else had happened since—break-ins or sexually. That last one was Cal's fault. Touching Mara messed with his head. He'd let his control slip. Now, he thought about her nonstop, and his headaches were back with a vengeance. Control was everything. He needed to find it again.

Mara stopped him outside her trailer. "Do you mind standing outside the door so no one barges in?" She winked as she asked the question, reminding him again how well she knew him.

Cal tried hiding his relief. "Anything you need," Cal said, closing the door behind Mara before turning his back to it and standing guard.

Five minutes in, he thought he might survive the pain. Then a balding man turned the corner, nearly colliding with Cal. He scurried to a stop. His hazel gaze met Cal's and the man's eyes widened in surprise. "Calhoun Walsh. Wow. What brings you here? I haven't seen you in what...a year?"

Cal bit back a groan. He honestly hadn't considered he might run into someone who knew him on set. "Hi, Samuel. I'm here—"

"He's here with me," Mara said behind him, making him wonder how long she'd been standing there.

Samuel sounded as surprised as he looked when he spoke. "Really? How do you two know each other?" he asked, motioning between them.

Mara laced her arm through Cal's. "Kieran Steele introduced us."

"Ah," Samuel said, his features clearing. "That makes sense. Kieran knows everyone."

"They're waiting for you, Mara," Michael said, appearing from nowhere the way he always did.

Cal swallowed back a sigh of relief. He might make it through this after all.

Samuel nodded. "I'm due back to stage three. It was good seeing you again, Calhoun. Mara, it's always a pleasure." Samuel said some other things, but Cal was too busy dying inside to hear a word of it.

To Mara's credit, she waited until Samuel was out of sight before pouncing. "Calhoun Walsh. Isn't there a senator by that name?"

Cal kept his gaze locked straight ahead as he walked her back to the set with Michael on their heels. "There is. My father." He fucking hated this.

"I thought his son was some sort of war hero who spent over a year as a POW before killing one of the top members of some terrorist organization. Didn't they make a movie about him?"

"Yes," Cal said through clenched teeth. Cold sweat broke out across Cal's forehead.

"Well," Mara said, sounding sad, "I have to hand it to you. You never called me a whiny bitch for complaining about my problems."

Cal glanced behind him. "Michael, I'll make sure Mara gets there in just a minute."

Michael looked up from his phone. Cal didn't know what Michael saw in Cal's face, but he didn't argue. Instead, he walked ahead, leaving them alone. Cal pulled Mara between two trailers where they were out of sight. The moment he had her attention, Cal held her gaze. "There's nothing small about anything you've gone through, and I would never trivialize you."

Mara's mouth lifted in one corner and he wished he could read her thoughts. When she finally spoke, butterflies stirred in his stomach. "You're pretty amazing. You know that, right?"

"I didn't do anything special. All I did was survive."

Mara waved away his words. "I'm not talking about the war hero stuff. Although that's massive. I meant you. You're amazing."

Before Mara, Cal had not only thought he'd never care about anyone again, he'd been scared to try. She was perfect for him. He didn't stand a chance against her.

"I want to kiss you, but I can't mess up Candy's work."

Mara winked. "Later."

Cal's mouth went dry at the thought. "Yes, ma'am."

He didn't know where they were headed. Maybe after today, she'd never think of him again, but Cal would think of her, and he wanted as many memories as he could get.

MARA SAID HER LINES, stood where she was told to stand, and focused where directed. In truth, she didn't know how she made it through the day. She'd seen the movie based on Cal's life. It had gutted her and left her feeling empty for days. When he'd told her he'd been in the military and had a prosthetic, her first thought had been IED. No. Cal had been chopped bit by bit. He'd been tortured in ways Mara couldn't stomach. Tears pressed at the backs of her eyes. Her stomach churned. He'd admitted to sleeping with the light on with shame in his voice. If it were her, she might not ever sleep again. He'd seen things and done things she'd couldn't even imagine. Things she couldn't fix. He hadn't wanted her to know. She couldn't unlearn the truth. That didn't mean she had to give in to the temptation to treat him differently. It didn't mean she was any less anxious to have him alone.

It wasn't until they headed down the dark road to her house that the truth slammed into her. He might never speak to her again. Cal was under no obligation to ever see her again. He didn't work for her. They'd wrapped up filming. It was possible they were over.

Before Mara knew what she was doing, her fears filled the air. "I can't believe you don't work for me any longer. It's just now really hit me. Come tomorrow, I won't see your face anymore. That breaks my heart. I guess I knew—"

Cal jerked the SUV to the side of the road, causing Mara's speech to die on her lips. She watched in stunned silence as Cal jumped from the vehicle, slamming the door behind him as he went. His every step screamed his rage. The muscles in his jaw jumped. The passenger side door flew open. Mara didn't have time to ask what was wrong. Cal was everywhere. His tongue brushed hers. The seatbelt disappeared. Mara held on to his shoulders while he squeezed her body against his with one arm. His free hand dove beneath her skirt. She didn't have time to think. Cal's kiss was like getting punched in the mouth by heaven. He bit and licked. The man was every bit as rough as she'd expected him to be the first time he'd touched her. He stroked her clit. Cal was ruthless. He didn't ease or coax her. This man demanded her pleasure. His large fingers stretched her wide. Mara rode them without shame. A mewling sound came from the back of her throat. She didn't give a fuck. In mere seconds, he had her ready to fly apart. She licked his tongue, savoring the taste of peppermint lingering there. He was fucking amazing—like an act of god overtaking her. Tension coiled in her gut. Her muscles tensed. She reached for what Cal offered, rocking against his hand. She knew she soaked his fingers. Mara could hear him touching her. The pressure building inside her snapped. She cried out and Cal swallowed the sound. Spasms rocked her. Before her head had time to clear, a larger pressure pushed its way inside her. Mara had to take a breath. Even as wet as she was for him, Cal was fucking huge. She couldn't think. All she could do was feel. He rocked against her. A moan vibrated against her lips. The tension built inside her again. She grabbed the handle on the ceiling and held on, as Cal buried himself deep. Mara spread her thighs and ground against him—like a crazed woman taking her pleasure.

Cal's mouth moved to her collarbone. His harsh breaths brushed her skin as he tugged her dress down, baring her breast. Cal's tongue stroked her nipple. Another orgasm slammed into her without warning. Mara threw her head back and rode the waves. Cal was silent—like a thief, stealing what he wanted. His fingers dug into her skin. He slammed home, making her cry out. Damn, she wanted everything he could give her. She'd been so fucking empty for so goddamn long. All she'd known was pain and helpless rage. Cal gave her life. Made her heart beat again. Tomorrow, she'd probably regret a thousand things about this moment. Right now, fuck all. She didn't care.

Cal's motions quickened. Mara held on. His lips found hers. Their tongues battled as his muscles hardened. It was so fucking sexy. Mara relished every second.

"Mara," he whispered against her lips as he came. She could feel his cock jerking inside her. A pant escaped. She'd never had a sexier moment with anyone. Cal was rough and raw—unforgiving. To her bones, she craved him. Not just his body—him. His time and silent strength. His heated glances, occasional evilness, and intelligence. Her arms tightened around him as their kiss softened. Come tomorrow, she'd probably never see him again. She hadn't been lying earlier. Her heart would be broken. In the three months he'd been with her, she'd come to depend on his presence. Mara didn't want to lose him. His gentle kiss screamed he was already gone.

Cal pulled out and warm liquid followed. Everything inside Mara froze.

Cal covered his eyes. "Fuck." He leaned in and dropped his forehead to Mara's shoulder. "Fuck," he repeated, sounding broken and stabbing Mara in the heart. "I'm so sorry. I don't know... I just... Fuck. I'm clean, and I can't have kids, because of you know... injuries. Goddamn, Mara. I wasn't thinking. I don't know what happened."

Mara was dying inside, but Cal was on the edge of losing his shit. She couldn't let that happen. He meant too much. She'd been as much to blame. Mara stroked his back and shushed him, hoping to keep him calm. She swore she could feel his internal freak out building into a real and physical thing. His muscles tensed and relaxed—like even he wasn't sure what he'd do. Mara couldn't let it take life. She was afraid—if she did—he'd never recover.

"It's okay, sweetie. Don't worry. I'm clean too, and even if you could have kids, I'm on the pill." She gently pushed him away so she could focus on his face and he could see her earnestness. Mara stroked his face, calming him like a wild animal. She rubbed the line between his eyes, smoothing it out before tracing his eyebrows. "You're so beautiful. Sometimes I want to stare at you all day." He didn't respond, but his muscles relaxed. "It's not fair for a man to have such perfect eyebrows," Mara said, stroking his brow again. "I bet you never even touch them." She ran her finger down his nose. "Terror chokes me at the thought of never seeing you again. How crazy is that? I don't know how it happened." The way Cal stared at her screamed he hung on every word. She knew his freak out had more to do with losing control than a condom. He needed her to be the strong one for once. She traced his lips. "I think about you more than I should." Cal lightly kissed her fingertips. Mara breathed past the flutter the pressure of his lips caused. "Thank you for being you, because you're exactly what I need."

Cal leaned in. Mara didn't stop toying with his lips until he gently pushed her hand aside and captured her lips. This time, his kiss was gentle—more like the ones they'd shared before. Mara realized something. The hard and rough Cal—the one who'd fucked her—was the real Cal. This gentle version was him in control, while he held the reins tight. She wanted both. If there was any forgiveness left in the universe for her sins, she prayed she could hang on to this one beautiful thing.

"Are you doing anything this weekend?" Cal asked against her lips.

Mara bit back a laugh. It was like their night happened in reverse—have sex and then ask for a date. "I think I'm free."

"I'm going to see my parents. Would you go with me?"

She didn't even need to think about it. "I'd love to meet your parents."

It was only one more weekend with Cal, but she'd take it. Mara had already decided—she'd take what time she could with Cal. One weekend at a time. No expectations. Only hope.

MARA MIGHT'VE BEEN LYING JUST a little when she'd said she'd love to meet Cal's parents. It wasn't that she didn't want to meet them. It was more that she was convinced a senator would not only be intimidating but would also hate her. Tracy and Calhoun Walsh were a formidable couple. Mara had seen the senator on the news many times, fighting for different causes or being interviewed about his stance on certain topics. His wife was often at his side at events and looked as stylish—if not more so—than many of the celebrities Mara knew. None of those glimpses into their lives prepared Mara for the real version of them.

They were farmers. Mara hadn't known that. Luckily, Cal had warned her to dress casually and pack to fit the same. She loved the country life and had no qualms about mucking around on a farm. Mara just hadn't been mentally prepared for the vast differences between the Calhoun she saw on TV and the real thing. He wore overalls. Mara couldn't understand why that fucked with her mind, but it did. The man wasn't the first farmer she'd met, but damned if she'd never really seen a farmer in overalls. They both refused to let her call them by anything other than their first names. Mara understood now the frustration she caused Cal by constantly insisting he call her by her name. She felt rude as hell every time she called his mother Tracy. It felt unnatural on her tongue. The stylish woman she'd seen on TV at Calhoun's side was also gone. The skinny brown-haired woman wore a cotton sundress and white canvas shoes. She also had a tendency to wear an apron, for fuck's sake. Mara felt like she'd stepped into an alternate universe where the fifties still raged on.

Cal was a perfect mixture of his parents. He had his mother's dark hair and his father's light blue eyes. Mara desperately wanted the pair to like her. By the time they made it to dessert of their first meal together, Mara still couldn't decide if they did.

"So, Mara," Tracy said, smiling. "I know what you do, but what do you do?"

Since the question confused the fuck out of Mara, she was more than a little relieved when Cal answered for her. "Filming takes almost seventeen hours a day, so..."

"That's a lot," Tracy said, looking impressed. "I'm glad you found time to join Cal this weekend."

"I just wrapped up a project, so it was no big deal. Even if I'd been busy, I would've made time. I've wanted to meet you both for a while." Damn, another lie. Oh, well.

Cal nodded. "She's always pushing me to visit."

Tracy perked up at that.

Mara wanted to kiss him.

"Where do your parents live?" Tracy asked between bites of pecan pie.

"I only have a mother and she passed a couple of years ago," Mara said, hoping she could leave it at that.

"So you're an orphan?'

Mara pushed her hair behind her ear, feeling more uncomfortable by the moment. "I suppose."

"You should come to this charity event tonight. They're raising money for orphans."

"It's for cancer," Calhoun corrected, sounding disinterested.

"Cancer. Orphans. Whatever. Your presence might help raise awareness and Cal being there would help as well."

"I told her to dress casual," Cal said before Mara could.

His mom waved off his words. "I can find her something, and you've got plenty of dress blues here."

"What type of project did you just wrap up?" Calhoun asked, changing the subject and saving Cal from what looked to soon become an argument. Talk of her upcoming movie carried them through pie. Cal's dad disappeared the moment dishes started getting loaded in the sink. Mara stayed glued to Tracy's side, determined to help.

Tracy shooed her away. "You're a guest. Go sit in the sunshine and enjoy the fresh air. I'm sure you're sick of the city's pollution."

Mara had nothing.

Cal laughed. "Mara lives out in the middle of nowhere. The city air isn't getting to her."

Tracy shrugged. "Still, she's on vacation. You're not," she said, handing Cal a dish towel. "You get to dry."

"I don't mind helping," Mara said for the tenth time.

Tracy waved her away. "Go sit down."

Mara caught Cal's eye as she slipped from the room. He winked. She bit back a smile. A sigh of relief rose in her throat the second she was alone. Taking Tracy's advice, Mara stepped outside. She followed the wraparound porch until she came to a set of rocking chairs. Mara wasn't the type to be uncomfortable in new situations. This was different for some reason. Important. Her shoulders hurt from being tense for too long. She hoped she could hide for at least ten minutes before returning to the strain. Mara chose the chair with the most shade. As Mara leaned back in the rocker, Tracy's voice floated from the nearby window, freezing Mara. After sneaking a peek over her shoulder, Mara realized her chair was just out of sight of the open window above the kitchen sink. She didn't want to eavesdrop, but she couldn't stop herself from hearing every word being said inside. "She's beautiful."

"She is," Cal agreed, making Mara smile.

"She's also an actress." The way Tracy said "actress"—like the word left a bad taste in her mouth—left no doubt it wasn't a profession the woman cared for.

Cal laughed. The sound warmed Mara's heart. "Yes, she's that too."

Tracy released a loud sigh. "Well, it's good to see you smiling again, but an actress."

Mara bit back a groan. It wasn't the first time in her life someone had looked down on her profession. As ridiculous as Mara found it to be, there were still people who didn't think acting was real work, or even worse, they still had the backwoods belief that actresses were the equivalent of whores. Damn it, she wanted Cal's parents to like her. She was starting to think it wouldn't happen.

Silence filled the kitchen, and Mara fought the urge to peek through the window like a proper weirdo. Cal finally spoke before her nerves snapped. "She's also a good person. I mean, to her core—good. She helps people, cares about them, and works nonstop at trying to make the world a better place. The world is ugly. It needs more people like her, and I don't feel quite so fucked up when she's around. I love you, and I'm sorry, but I can't care what you think about her profession or any other aspect of her life. This isn't about you."

Mara's lips parted in surprise. She didn't want his mom to hate her, but she'd also never had anyone sound so proud of being with her. The backs of Mara's eyes burned.

"I just want you to be happy," Tracy said, cutting into Mara's rush of emotions. "My point is you'll probably have to fight off a lot of men to keep someone like her."

"Women too," Cal said. Mara could hear the smile in his voice. "I'm not afraid."

"Would you walk with me?" Mara startled at Calhoun's

sudden appearance. She tried not to show her guilt over listening to Cal and Tracy's conversation. Instead, Mara stood and accepted the elbow Calhoun offered—like a proper gentleman.

"Of course."

He headed toward the lake in the center of their land. Mara matched his slow pace. Mara couldn't deny they had a beautiful spread. Cal had mentioned on the flight they had over two hundred acres. Mara searched for anything to talk about. "This place is gorgeous."

"Thank you." He sounded stern and distant.

The air held its breath. She could feel the man's thoughts brewing, and she got the impression he never spoke without first weighing every word. A true politician. She bit back a groan when he finally broke the silence. "I had you checked out before you came here."

Mara faked a small chuckle. "I don't imagine you had to dig hard. My life is out there for everyone to see."

Calhoun didn't look her way. "It wasn't you the actress I was concerned with. I wanted to know more about you the person."

"Did you learn anything good?"

He didn't respond right away. Mara's stomach twisted into knots. She didn't have a lot of secrets, but the ones she had, she wouldn't want shared with Cal's parents. "You do a lot of humanitarian work."

"As one should when they're more fortunate than others," Mara said without hesitation.

"I hear you also claimed the bodies of two of your ex-employees after a murder-suicide incident."

Wow. There it was. He didn't waste any time with small talk. Mara refused to let her steps falter. For some reason she couldn't explain, Mara couldn't let this man see her as weak. "I did," Mara said, surprising herself with how steady she sounded. "Landon didn't have life insurance and his family couldn't afford to bury him, so I did. Early's family refused to claim her body after what she'd done. They were more than happy with me taking care of her."

Calhoun stopped by the edge of the lake. He finally looked over and met her gaze. "You sound like you feel as if you did the right thing despite the scandal it could've caused."

Mara hardened her voice. Fuck a scandal when talking about people losing their lives. "I don't *feel* like I did the right thing. I *know* I did. Sometimes people are struggling with things no one else can see or understand. What happened was horrible and can never be undone, but—in my eyes—it doesn't take away from how beautiful Early was until that final bad decision."

To her surprise, Calhoun smiled. "It's good to hear that conviction in your voice. I worried my son might be just another act of charity or a way to make you look like a better person in the media. Plus, it'll take a strong woman to handle the man who came home, and I imagine you could have anyone you want."

It had been a test. She wanted to be angry and insulted, and she was. Just not for herself. "You're right. I can have anyone I want." Mara left it to Calhoun to judge her words. He could take it as conceit, if he chose to do so, or he could be smart and realize Cal was who she wanted. "Being with Cal is the easiest thing I've ever done," Mara added, because she couldn't stop. "The man who came home is a damn good man."

Calhoun released a low chuckle. "I know. It's as you said—some people just struggle with things people can't see. Not everyone would be willing take that on, but your claiming those bodies proves you're not like most people." Mara realized Calhoun was trying to show his approval of her. She didn't know what to say.

Thankfully, Cal appeared, saving her. "Please tell me Dad's not telling you the story of the time I almost drowned out here."

"You got here just in time," Calhoun said, sounding bright. "I was just about to start." Before Cal could stop him, Calhoun fell into the story of Cal sneaking out to go skinny dipping with some girl down the road and ending up getting CPR from an EMT with his dick out.

Mara listened with half an ear, laughing in all the appropriate places. It was hard to pay attention with Cal wrapping her in his arms. His hard chest pressed against her back. He kissed the top of her head several times. Mara couldn't stop smiling. She felt loved. Her heart skipped a beat at the thought. She'd been wrong in the past. What if she was a show to make his parents worry less? Mara held tighter to Cal's arms. She'd reached for more in the past, only to get slapped down. Mara wouldn't do it this time. She'd take whatever Cal offered and it would be enough— no matter what, because her heart wasn't strong enough for another break yet. Even if Cal didn't mean his touches, she didn't feel broken when he held her. It was enough.

"I see the two of you are only humoring me until you can be alone, so I'll head inside."

"No, please stay," Mara said, feeling bad for letting her mind wander.

Cal covered her mouth. "Don't listen to her. The heat is frying her brain." Mara licked his palm. He didn't move his hand away.

Calhoun shook his head and laughed. "I've got to get ready for a fund-raising thing I have tonight anyhow. You two have fun, but not so much we have to call the paramedics."

Mara tried responding.

Cal still wouldn't let her. "See you later, Dad."

Mara balled up her fist and punched him in the thigh. Cal grunted but still didn't release her until his father was gone. The moment they were alone, he dropped his hand. Before she could give him a piece of her mind, he spun her in his arms and kissed her. Her irritation fell away as his tongue brushed hers. By the time he pulled away, she couldn't remember why she'd been aggravated in the first place.

"Do you fish, Miss King?"

Mara straightened her spine. "Sir, I am a Louisiana girl to my bones," Mara said, using her thickest country accent. "Not only do I fish, but I won the Louisiana freshwater American bass tournament when I was twelve."

Cal's laughter was beautiful. "Jesus. You're something else. Come on," he said, leading her toward the boathouse.

"I'm being serious," Mara argued, matching his pace. "It was a thirteen-hundred-dollar prize. I bought a purse."

Cal's steps faltered. He glanced her way, looking disbelieving. "One purse?"

Mara nodded. "It was a nice purse." She thought about it for a second. "I can't remember what happened to it. In truth, it was the ugliest thing I'd ever seen, but I'd heard it was the latest thing." Mara kept talking as Cal gathered rods and reels from the boat house and loaded them on the boat sitting at the pier. "I was a tomboy and didn't care about name brand anything unless it was bowling balls, because I loved to bowl. Anyhow, Chandra Grey, she was the class idol, she always had the nicest handbags and everyone thought she was the shit. She was dating the boy I liked. I use the word dating loosely, because—you know—we were kids. Really, they just sat together at lunch, and I wanted him to sit with me. But I got it in my head, I would win this contest and buy this purse, then he would like me and not her."

Cal stopped what he was doing to focus on Mara, as if invested in her story. "And did he like you better than her once he saw your purse?"

A smile exploded across Mara's face at the memory. "Yes, but only because it turned out he was gay and it really was all about the handbag. He's still my best friend. Oh," Mara said, her story making her realize something important. "It's just occurred to me you haven't met Chase. We became best friends in school, but then he moved away. In a twist of fate, we both got famous and have starred in a few movies together."

Cal looked confused for a second. "Chase Freeman? I didn't know he was gay. Not that it matters," he tacked on. "I just thought he'd been dating some actress for a long time."

Mara snorted. "That actress was me, and no, we never dated. He's married to an Olympic snowboard champion. Has been for years."

Cal helped Mara into the boat. "Huh. I guess I haven't been keeping up with my celebrity gossip."

Mara shrugged as she claimed a seat. "You're not missing anything."

Cal climbed in before focusing on her. "I don't know if that's true. Seems like I missed a lot of years I could've been stalking you."

Mara tried her damnedest to squelch a smile. He always said the best things. She loved it. After steering them out into the water, far enough where they could still see the roof of the house, Cal killed the engine. While Mara looked on, he cast out two lines and set the rods in the rod holders.

Mara couldn't stop her laughter. Not only had he not used bait, he hadn't used anything. Cal simply tossed out an empty line. "It's been a while, but I'm pretty sure that's not how you catch a fish."

Cal settled onto the floor of the boat before pulling her off her seat and in between his knees. She rested her back against his chest as he wrapped her in his arms. His lips touched he shell of her ear. Mara's eyes fell closed. She loved these moments. "We're not fishing," he admitted against her ear. "If I know my mom, since we're not married, we won't be sharing a room. If I want you alone, this is the only way I'll have it."

"I like the way your mind works."

Cal's lips skimmed across her ear again. "If my dad dragged you out here to grill you, I'm sorry. He's a politician. He spends a lot of time with liars."

Mara's eyes were too heavy to open. She tried memorizing every nuance. "He's a dad. It's his job to make sure I'm good enough for you. If my mom was still alive, she would've had a background check waiting—complete with an annual earnings statement. She was brutal about protecting me."

Cal's hand slid up her body until his fingers encircled her throat. He gently held her in place as sucked her lobe between his teeth. Mara's nipples hardened. Her breath caught and a tingle began between her legs. His mouth on her skin was all it took. "I'll get those things together for you, if you'd like."

"What things?" Mara asked, losing the threads of their conversation.

Cal's low chuckle rumbled against her skin and Mara

fought the urge to moan. His hand moved from her throat, slipping down her body. "I wonder if you're already wet for me." She could answer, but she was willing to let him find out for himself. "These are cute shorts," Cal said, tugging at the strings of her yellow cotton shorts. "Do you know what I like about them?"

"What?" Even to Mara's ears, she sounded breathless. "The waistband is stretchy," he answered as he dipped his hand inside. Mara's lips parted on a pant when Cal cupped her sex. "Damn, you are wet for me."

Mara fought the urge to grind herself against his palm. "Always."

One finger dipped inside her. Cal sucked in a ragged breath, as if her pleasure was his. "Of all the sexual acts I've seen over the years, this is the hottest. I can't see what my hand is doing, beyond a bulge in your shorts, but I can feel you. You're an image in my head. I can picture your flushed skin and wet folds. It's almost as if your clit is on my tongue." He found the nub he described and rubbed. A whimper came from the back of Mara's throat. "That's it, baby. I can make you feel good."

Mara gripped his thighs and hung on. "You always make me feel good just by existing."

Cal played with her clit. His other arm tightened around her. "It's like you always know what to say to hit me in the chest. I don't have the words you do. All I have is an insatiable need to touch you, and even though I want you, it's not lust driving me. It's something else. Something more intense."

Damn, that sounded a lot like love and Mara was scared to dream anyone might love her. She'd been unloved too long. At the very least, most people had a parent to love them. Mara had no one. She was in front of the world—

alone. Cal's words made her dream about a different life. The way he circled her clit, teasing her, kept her from thinking too hard about anything other than the orgasm he sought to steal. "I love the way you touch me."

Cal kissed the spot beneath her ear and increased the speed of his fingers. Against her will, Mara's hips rose. She moved against his hand, seeking relief. "Damn, that's sexy, Mara. That tiny sound you make—like I'm showing you heaven—I live for it. It makes me want to be better so I can hear it all the time."

Mara had a feeling she should be arguing some points, but her body's needs wouldn't let her focus. Her muscles were taut and pleasure felt just out of reach. An invisible spring wound tight inside her, ready to snap. She squeezed her breasts, seeking relief from the tension. Just as she thought she'd fly apart, Cal froze. A whimper escaped. She wanted to scream.

"I'm picturing this is my tongue," Cal whispered against her ear as he dragged his finger tip down her nub. An orgasm slammed into Mara, making her channel pulse and her legs shake. Her breaths came in gasps as Cal rubbed out every last twitch from Mara, leaving her a useless mess. Her muscles were like gelatin. She couldn't move. In her head, she did everything she could to please Cal the way he had her. In reality, she couldn't force her body to work.

"I promise, the second I can use my arms and legs, I'll make you fly."

Cal's low chuckle against her neck sent another aftershock through her. "You're making me fly now by letting me hold you. Let me have this."

No one had ever messed with her head the way Cal did. He genuinely didn't want anything else from her right now. She could hear it in his voice. Mara didn't understand him.

He wasn't like anyone she'd ever met before. She'd been through a lot in the past year and a half. Nothing had killed her yet. If Cal walked away, she didn't know if that would still be true.

———————

MARA'S HEARTBEAT raced beneath his palm. He held tight, needing to feel the rapid drum. She made him feel alive. His leaking cock screamed for her touch, but it wasn't as loud as the voice in his head, yelling at him to confess his love. It was too soon. He didn't think she'd accept it, and he was already too intense. Cal didn't want to scare her away. His mind already had only a thin layer of glue holding the pieces together. If Mara walked away, what would she leave behind? He couldn't think about it.

"It's so peaceful here. What made you decide to move to New Orleans rather than staying here when you came home?"

It was funny how Cal never considered not answering any of Mara's personal questions. All the things he didn't want to talk about were easy when he was with her. Plus, she gave him something to focus on other than his raging hard on. He'd take it. "I did stay here for a while, helping out around the farm while healing. It didn't take long, though, for people to start contacting me about book deals and movie deals. Obviously, I didn't know anything about any of that. Someone mentioned Kieran, saying I needed an agent, so I looked him up. Of course, I didn't know he was a sports agent, but he still asked to me to come to New Orleans. I went and got to know Henley and him." The words flowed from Cal—like he'd been waiting for someone to ask. "They were a lifeline in a way. I swear

Kieran took one look at me and knew I wasn't doing as well as I pretended. They were really open and honest. Henley told me about his past troubles with addiction, and how he almost died from an overdose before meeting Kieran. He shared some secrets with me about coping. I realized I was better in New Orleans, away from people who care too much and watch me all the time, expecting me to fall apart at any second. The truth is, I was already falling apart every second. It was just happening on the inside where they couldn't see." Mara stroked his arms, making him feel loved, and Cal kept confessing everything. "I told Kieran I didn't care a whole lot about how much money I got, but I wanted him to represent me. He laughed and asked if I really thought I could go back to working a normal job someday. I knew I couldn't. He promised he'd ensure I would never have to work again. Thanks to him dealing on my behalf, I can be a basket case in private until the end."

"Yet you still took the job with me."

It hadn't been a question, but it was the second time Mara had brought it up. He couldn't leave her remark without acknowledgement. "When you were on the phone, telling me when and where to report, you had the same panic in your voice I feel every day. I couldn't ignore it. You know I'm not better, right? I might not ever be."

Mara didn't respond right away.

Panic built in his chest. Cal didn't want to scare her away. He also didn't want her to have any illusions about his mental health.

"It hurts my heart to think of you silently falling apart," Mara finally said. Her tone matched her claim. "But I'm not hanging around, hoping for a better or different version of you. I just want you. We're a matched set," she said, making him smile. "Just a little chipped and frayed around the edges, but perfect together."

He couldn't hold her tight enough to soothe his heart. They couldn't stay out there, hiding all day. "Would you like to be my date to a charity event tonight?"

"I'd be your date anywhere, Mr. Walsh."

He hoped that was true, because he didn't plan to ever let her go.

CHAPTER NINE

T hree months later...

"I'VE GOTTEN five calls in the last twenty-four hours, asking for comments from you about your relationship with Cal."

Mara rolled her eyes at Michael's remark. "You'd think one public charity event over three months ago equated sex on the table for the world to see. Sheesh. Don't they have anything better to talk about yet? Hasn't anyone gotten a DUI or publicly flipped their shit lately? Come on, Hollywood. You're failing me."

"Not a single boob falling out in public either. Pity."

Mara snorted at Michael's bland tone. "What do you care about boobs?"

"Not a thing," Michael said before seeming to reconsider. "Other than they make for fun news."

"What makes for fun news?" Cal said, returning from the kitchen with a glass of wine for Mara and a bottle of water for himself. Damn, she loved the sight of him relaxed as he was tonight. Loose-fit jeans and cotton long-sleeve shirt. It had a row of four buttons at the collar. He'd left two undone, showing just enough skin to make her want to lick him.

"Boobs," Michael said, answering Cal's question and dragging Mara's mind back on topic.

"What do you care about boobs?" Cal asked, using the exact tone she had moments earlier. Mara and Michael exchanged a glance before bursting into laughter.

"Okay," Cal said, sounding lost. He handed Mara the wineglass and claimed the empty spot next to her on the couch. Mara's stomach churned as the smell of wine overcame her. She set the glass aside. Cal eyed her face. "Are you okay? You look a little pale."

She flashed him a smile. "I'm fine. Just feeling a little off. I think I'll stick to water tonight."

Cal passed his unopened water bottle her way and moved as if to stand again. "Do you need anything else?"

Mara stopped him from getting back up. "I'm fine." She passed the water back to him. "Do you need anything else? I'll get up this time." She stood before he could argue. They room spun a little, but she refused to show it. Mara never got sick.

"I'm good," Cal said, staring at her as if he wasn't fooled.

She headed for the kitchen before he saw too much.

Michael trailed along on her heels. "Do I need to set up a doctor's appointment for you?" he asked the moment they were out of earshot.

"I just need some water," Mara said, flashing him a smile. "And a keeper. I'm such a dumbass. It just occurred to me I haven't really had anything to drink all day," she added, turning up a bottle of water, attempting to prove her point.

"I am your keeper," Michael reminded her. "Now, do I need to set up a doctor's appointment for you?"

Mara sighed. He wasn't going to let it go. "Do whatever you want. What's up with you?" she asked, changing the subject. "You seem sad."

"I'm not sad, but I am about to head out for the night. Go to sleep," he ordered, sounding stern. "You look exhausted, which is ridiculous considering you're not working right now. Stop staying up all night worrying over your man not sleeping, and let the man not sleep. You can't fall for someone dark and brooding, and then fret when they turn out to be dark and brooding."

Michael's description of her current woes was too apt for Mara to keep a straight face. A chuckle escaped her before dying on a sigh. "Come here," she said, waving Michael closer. "Give me a hug, and don't tell me you don't need one, because it's written all over your face." A low growl escaped Michael, but he dutifully gave her hug. When his arms came around her, he held on tighter than she expected, proving her point. To her surprise, Mara's eyes filled with tears. It wasn't uncommon for her to get emotional, but it was unexpected under the circumstances. Mara didn't let go. "You'd tell me if you needed me, right?" she asked in a low voice, needing him to know they were friends above all else.

"Of course," Michael said, pulling away, and Mara knew he lied. It was written in every syllable of his fake tone. "Now go to bed," Michael ordered again, giving her a stern look before heading for the door. Mara watched him go and worried at her bottom lip. He could protest all he wanted, but Mara knew something was going on with him.

"That's a good idea."

Mara's gaze shot to the doorway of the kitchen. Cal stood with his shoulder leaned against the frame. "What's a good idea?"

Cal's mouth turned up in one corner, as if amused by her. "You should go to bed. It's obvious you're not feeling well."

"I feel fine." It was true. Whatever had been making her head swim earlier had passed. Now Cal had the bedroom on her mind. "If you want me to go to bed, you should make me." Mara couldn't keep the taunt from her voice.

Cal didn't bother arguing. He simply crossed the room and lifted her into his arms. Mara curled up against his chest and stared at his face as he carried her to the bedroom. He had the sexiest jawline. She wanted to kiss it. Mara was so damn warm and happy in Cal's arms. When he set her on the mattress, she clung to his shirt, refusing to let him get away. His light-blue gaze collided with hers. Mara's breath caught in the back of her throat at his intensity. Michael had been right earlier. She had fallen for Cal. Sometimes, when he looked at her, as he did now, she knew he felt the same. But the words always froze in her throat before falling from her lips. Mara had already learned the hard way once that—sometimes—what she thought other people felt for her, didn't really exist at all. How much longer would she get with him until he ripped everything away from her, the way everyone always did?

"You look sad," Cal said, setting one knee on the mattress and straddling her body. He kept his weight braced on his palms and knees, but there was no way she could move him. Mara was pinned beneath his large frame and piercing stare.

"I'm not," Mara promised. Maybe a small part of her

was, but he wasn't gone yet. She still had time to savor him. "Kiss me."

The instant Cal lowered his head and touched his lips to hers, Mara shoved her hands underneath his shirt, going for bare skin. His breath shuddered against her lips as he teased her lips open. Goddamn, his every reaction was addictive. No one else had ever reacted to her touch the way he did—like she moved him. Cal repositioned his body until she cradled him at the apex of her thighs. His erection ground against her through her clothes. He wasn't soft. Cal's tongue demanded entry. He licked at the inside of her mouth, making her pant. He rocked against her at the perfect angle. Her panties were soaked. She wanted them gone. Mara wasn't one to ask permission. She popped the button on Cal's jeans and pushed them down his hips as far as she could without help. Cal's mouth moved to her throat. He shoved at her clothes, pushing her shirt higher and her cotton shorts lower. Her back arched as she sought his touch. Cal's patience seemed to disappear. He tore at her clothes, pulling them from her body with little to no grace. She didn't care. Mara wanted them gone. She craved what only Cal could give her.

Mara pushed at his chest, forcing him to give her room to set his erection free. She no longer cared that she was nude while he was still almost completely dressed. Mara wanted him inside her, making her feel more than alive. When it came to sex, Cal was never gentle. Mara loved it. She knew it meant she'd stolen the control he held too tightly. She wanted his tongue on her skin. His teeth denting her flesh. She needed to feel like he was hers, and she wasn't alone in this sickness inside her.

There was no prep work. It wasn't needed. She was always ready for Cal. He shoved her knee higher and pushed his way inside. Mara held her breath and focused on the way he hit everything at the perfect angle. Everything else disappeared. She was nothing more than want and need. Cal kissed her so deeply, she could barely breathe. She didn't need oxygen—only him. Her muscles tightened around his cock, attempting to keep him inside as his dick sawed in and out. He reached between them and toyed with her clit, stealing a moan from her throat. Mara's hips lifted, trying to get closer—to take everything she craved. Her muscles screamed from being tensed—balanced on the edge of release. She focused on Cal's touch, reaching for what he offered. Light burst inside her and the pressure broke, sending wave after wave of ecstasy rolling through her.

Mara bit Cal's bottom lip as she whimpered and he dragged her pleasure out as long as possible. He pulled away and pressed his forehead to hers. Mara stared at his face, marveling at the way he kept his eyes squeezed shut and his lips parted as he pumped inside her, reaching for his own release. The moment his orgasm hit, Cal's eyes opened and their gazes met. The world stopped for Mara as they'd stared at each other—more connected than any two people in the world. She loved him. That was something that would never die.

Cal rolled to the side, but he didn't release her. Even as he grabbed a handful of comforter and pulled it over them, Cal didn't let go. She snuggled as close as she could get and stared at his flushed face. His eyes were closed and he fought to catch his breath. He was beautiful. Mara couldn't look away. Even as his breaths calmed and then deepened, Mara barely blinked. Soon, she'd let go. There was no other choice. It wouldn't be long before she'd have to be honest with him. She'd watch his expression close against her, and then he'd be gone. After all, Cal's "I can't be fixed" always sounded a lot like "this is temporary" to Mara. At least he was honest. Mara would eventually have to retreat to the solitude she'd had before him.

A whimper came from the back of Cal's throat—like a broken man. His muscles tensed, and she knew the nightmares had come, as they did every night. Mara did what she always did. She pet him. Starting at his head, she swiped her fingers through his hair, and then soothed her palm down his cheek. She stroked his chest and his arms until his muscles relaxed and the dreams went away, leaving him in peace.

Cal's mouth lifted in one corner, as if she'd transformed his nightmare into something good. The weight that lived on her chest since meeting Cal increased. She wanted to keep him. He belonged to her. Yet, he never would.

"Mara," he whispered as his eyes fluttered open.

The words that had been stuck in her throat, choking her, burst from her. "I love you."

Cal exploded into action, flying from the bed without a backward glance. He straightened his clothes as he went.

Mara watched it happen from her spot on the bed, incapable of moving. "Are you okay?" She had no idea how she managed to squeeze the question past her rapidly swelling throat.

Cal still didn't look her way. His frame was stiff and unbending. Even from Mara's position, she could see a muscle jumping in his jaw. "I need to think," he growled as he headed for the door.

Mara stared at the ceiling and didn't move. She wouldn't chase him. Once again, everything was her greedy heart's fault. He'd told her time and time again he couldn't be fixed. Every time she'd heard what he meant—don't get attached. Mara's heart didn't work that way. It got invested every time. Her heart craved and ached, demanding everything. Once again, it wanted more than someone else could give. She deserved to be alone.

Cal didn't return. She'd known he wouldn't. The alarm panel in her room had lit ten minutes earlier, showing his departure. Still, she didn't move. He'd ripped the comforter from her body in his escape. She was cold. Mara did nothing to remedy it. Cold and alone was a familiar state. She wrapped the emotions around her like a blanket. Twice now, she'd fallen in love. Both times, everything had shattered in a blink of an eye the moment she exposed her heart. This time was different. Soon, Michael would make that appointment for her. She'd be forced to face the truth. Soon, everything would change. It was best she get reacquainted with cold and alone. Soon, that would be all she had.

CAL WAS like a toy powered by a string. Mara had pulled his chain with her confession. Now, he couldn't stop moving. He'd stamped into his shoes, was out the door, and halfway down the road before he drew a breath. His brain wouldn't work at all. He'd woken from a nightmare with her pressed against him. Her sweet scent and familiar weight comforted him. He'd known before his eyes opened he was safe. She made him feel that way. Then, Mara had said the words he'd been warning her not to feel since they met.

He'd told her several times he couldn't be fixed. Cal would never be better. Now, he couldn't think. He'd left. Funny how that fact just now sank in. She'd told him she loved him, and Cal had left. Jesus. He barely stopped himself from punching himself right in the jaw. Of all the dumbass moves he could've made, that was the one he'd chosen. He needed to think. That part hadn't been a lie. Cal needed to turn this over in his mind until he no longer felt the taint of insanity. But leaving, fuck. That had been stupid as hell.

Unfortunately, he couldn't make himself turn back. Cal's foot refused to lift from the gas and his fists stayed steadily wrapped around the steering wheel, heading in the opposite direction of everything he wanted most. His heart screamed his home was behind him. Cal ignored that voice. If he went back, then he'd have to embrace the fact that Mara had chosen him—a broken down man with nothing to offer but a tarnished soul. If he turned back, he'd have to accept he loved her too, and that was a dick move. No one deserved that.

Cal kept his gaze locked straight ahead and blocked out his thoughts. He needed to regain control. Rather than heading home, Cal found his Chevy parked in the back lot of The Rabbit Warren, and his feet headed toward the door. His mind shied away from the place. Being here, it felt a lot like cheating. He felt... wrong. Those feelings didn't stop him from digging out his wallet and swiping his membership card at the door, unlocking it. His guilt didn't slow his step as he headed for the bar. The man in charge of services caught his eye and headed his way. Cal didn't flinch or back down.

"Are my play partners here?" Cal asked before he could change his mind. He needed control more than he needed to feel better about himself.

A line appeared between Mark's eyebrows at Cal's question. "Did they not tell you? They cancelled their membership. If you'd like, I could find you a different couple."

Kieran and Henley were through with this place. Cal couldn't say he was surprised. Something had seemed off the past few times he'd joined them. He stared at Mark, unsure of what to do. Cal needed to know he could control the most basic of instincts. He needed to pass this test again, as he had countless times with Kieran. But the truth was, he'd never been in any real danger of failing with Henley and Kieran, because they'd never let him join, even if his control had snapped. They weren't a threat to his heart. The pair had been a release without the consequences or touching. No one else could give him that, and only one person touched him.

"No, thank you," Cal said, amazed at how calm he sounded. Without another word, he turned away. He would cancel his membership as well. There was nothing left for him here. In truth, there was nothing left for him anywhere. He'd left his shattered mind back in a dark cave in the desert. His heart belonged to Mara. The rest of him walked around dead and without purpose. Cal had no idea where to go from here.

NEVER IN A MILLION YEARS—IF she'd ever thought about it—would Mara have thought Kieran would be the person she ran to in her time of need. Yet here she was, driving to his house. A chuckle kept rising in her throat. Mara couldn't decide if it was due to finding humor in her situation or if it was a hysterical one. She made her way past the gate and circled the house to park. Mara forced her mind blank. Overthinking things had led her here to begin with. Now it was time for her comeuppance.

To her surprise, Kieran's younger brother, Gannon,

answered the door. Seeing him made her smile. Looking at him made everyone smile. He was young, gorgeous, and sweet. His messy brown hair and cute blue eyes damn near made her blush. No man should be as pretty.

"Hey, Gannon. I didn't know you were visiting." She accepted his hug, still trying to find a way to apologize. "I guess I should've called first."

"Don't worry over it," Gannon said, giving her a light squeeze before releasing her. "This place is still like a second home to me. I'm here a lot, which you'd know if you visited more often," he said, sounding like his brother.

Mara flashed him an apologetic smile. "Sorry about that. Things have been insane. Is Kieran around?" She hoped she wasn't making Gannon feel brushed off, but she was scared she'd lose her nerve if she waited too long to talk to Kieran.

Gannon motioned toward a set of closed double doors off the living room. "He's in his office. I'd knock first since Henley is home, and you know..."

"Do you mean I know he's a dirty boy?" Mara snorted out a horrified laugh as the question floated from her mouth. She was so damn nervous she wasn't guarding her tongue.

Gannon's eyes flashed with humor. "That's exactly what I meant, so knock. It was good seeing you again," Gannon said, heading out the door and leaving her alone.

Mara spent a moment eyeing Kieran's expensive furnishings. He'd inherited this house. The man came from generations of money and old money bled from his pores. It only took one glance at the man's home to see it. If she'd never met the man, his antiques and polished wood would tell Kieran's story. Not all of it, though. Not the parts that made his heart golden. That was why she'd come here first and why she wouldn't give in to the temptation to race from the house. Instead, she put one foot in front of the other until her knuckles skimmed the wooden door of his office.

"Come."

Even though Kieran's tone was terse, Mara turned the knob and slipped inside. She smiled at the sight of him hunched over a stack of paperwork. "Oh, thank god. You yelled 'come' and I automatically opened the door. How embarrassing it would've been if you hadn't been speaking to me."

Kieran's bright smile doubled her belief she'd come to the right place. "Henley is being lazy by the pool, so you're good."

Mara crossed the room and claimed the chair across from him. "I heard he's retiring at the end of this season. Do you plan to join him in a life of leisure?"

"Who knows?" Kieran said evasively. "I kind of like helping people. I'm not sure I could stop."

There was the golden heart that had brought her here. He checked his watch. "Speaking of helping people, it's just occurred to me I've never opened the bottle of wine you sent for finding Cal. How's that going?"

"He quit."

Kieran's gaze shot to hers. "Really?"

Mara nodded. "About three and half months ago, right before filming ended. It's okay, though," she rushed to reassure him. "He kept me in contract." She chewed on her bottom lip. The fluttering in her stomach threatened to make her puke from nerves. "Actually, Cal is sort of why I stopped by. In a way."

Kieran opened his desk drawer, shifting through its contents. "Go on," he said, pulling out a cork screw.

Mara didn't know where to start. "Filming is over," she

said again unnecessarily. "But Cal and I aren't. Well, at least, I hope we're not. I don't know."

Kieran paused in his search through his drawers. "Was I supposed to get something from all that?"

Heat exploded through Mara's cheeks and she had no idea why. She felt like a teenager telling her parents she liked a boy. "We're a couple, I suppose."

"You suppose?" Kieran asked, sliding his chair to a nearby cabinet and swinging open the door. He came out with a bottle of wine and a glass.

"We are," she reaffirmed. "Or we were, and then I fucked things up—like I always do. But—"

"Then not only is it five o'clock somewhere, you need a stress reliever," Kieran said, interrupting her and holding up the glass. "Interested?"

"No, I—" The glass caught her eye, drawing her up short. It came from a one-of-a-kind set engraved for her by a Saudi prince as a gift for her thirtieth birthday. It was the glass that had gone missing the night she'd gone to The Rabbit Warren with Cal. Her gaze slid to Kieran's. His expression remained blank as he held out the glass to her. She noticed he held it carefully, with a cloth napkin around the stem, as if avoiding getting his fingerprints on the piece. "What did you do?"

Kieran didn't bat an eye. "We'd be here all day if I started listing my past transgressions. Would you like some wine?"

Mara couldn't respond. Her stare refused to budge from the wineglass Kieran had obviously stolen. She doubted he'd done it personally. More likely, he'd hired someone. She didn't know how to feel. Mara had come here because she trusted him and needed advice. Now she wondered if she trusted anyone. Kieran set the glass in front of her. She watched as he opened the bottle of wine she'd given him. When he moved as if to pour her some, Mara covered the glass with her hand, stopping him. She stood, picking up the glass as she went. Mara wondered if she looked as confused as she felt.

"I can't drink. I'm pregnant," Mara said, taking her wineglass and heading for the door. She didn't look back. If she'd shocked Kieran, then they were even, and she'd have to figure things out on her own.

CHAPTER TEN

I t was a damn good thing Henley had decided to retire. Kieran didn't know how much more he could stand of watching the man get hurt. He'd taken a skate to the thigh two nights ago and wouldn't be playing for the rest of the season. His husband's career ended—just like that and earlier than intended. Kieran hadn't stopped babying him since. With his man curled up on the couch in the corner, Kieran worked quietly at his desk while Henley slept. Despite the good he felt he'd done for Mara, guilt ate at Kieran. He didn't want to lose a friend. Sometimes, he forgot not everyone was as cutthroat as him. When it came to Henley, Kieran would stop at nothing. He forgot not everyone had that same intensity when it came to matters of the heart. Mara and Cal were obviously meant to be. It was apparent to anyone with eyes. All he'd done was give them a little push. It had worked too.

Unfortunately, he hadn't considered a pregnancy. Kieran couldn't see Cal handling that well. The man hadn't wanted to touch another adult. A defenseless child... Cal might not ever want anything to do with his baby. It was good Mara had run out on him. No doubt, that was why she'd come to Kieran in the first place—to hear what he thought. He couldn't be the one to tell her Cal probably wouldn't want this. So, once again, he was meddling.

Gannon poked his head in the door. "Hey," he said, keeping his voice low to keep from waking Henley. "Cal Walsh is here. He said you called him and asked him to come, but I didn't want to send him in here until I cleared it with you."

"Thanks. I called him earlier."

"Cool. I'll send him in."

Pride rose in Kieran's chest. Gannon might be his younger brother, but Kieran had raised him like a son. Every time he came to stay, and Kieran saw the amazing man he'd become, he couldn't get enough time with him. His house was overflowing with love. Gannon's husband, Alex, was there showering him with attention. Henley was no longer working and Kieran had everything.

Cal came through the door. There were dark circles underneath his eyes and he wore jeans in place of his usual expensive business suits. Although it was hot as hell out, long sleeves covered his arms. Kieran fought the urge to shake his head. It seemed even Mara's love hadn't convinced him to stop hiding his scars.

Cal's gaze moved to the corner of the room where Henley slept, making him wonder if Gannon had warned him to keep his voice low. "How's he feeling?" Cal asked quietly, proving Kieran's thoughts right.

"He's making it. They released him from the hospital early this morning. He's refusing pain meds, so... you know." Kieran hated to say more. Cal knew better than most that Henley was a recovering addict. They could plan for a lot of things, but this was one scenario they hadn't considered. Kieran hadn't felt so helpless in a long time.

"He has you," Cal said, sounding confident. "He'll be fine. So, what do you need my help with? I'm assuming that's why you called."

A smile tugged at the corners of Kieran's mouth. Cal was a good guy. Kieran hoped he wasn't about to lose another friend. "I hear congratulations are in order."

"Kieran," Henley said from the corner, sounding groggy as he chastised him. "Not our place."

Kieran's gaze shot in Henley's direction. He eyed his husband's pale face and checked for any signs of distress. Henley looked tired but otherwise okay, so Kieran didn't let the man's argument deter him. He'd set Cal and Mara up, hoping they'd end up right where they were. Well, maybe not right where they were. They weren't supposed to be stupid and apart. Kieran did his best to reassure Henley. "It has to be somebody's place, baby. If he freaks out, better he does it here. You know first reactions are everything. If he flips out in front of Mara, she'll be crushed and never forget it."

"What the fuck are you talking about?" Cal asked, sounding exhausted and irritated.

Kieran flashed him a bright smile. "Your congratulations. Surprise! You're going to be a dad."

Cal's expression went blank. "I'm sorry, what? Mara is on the pill and I was told I most likely couldn't have kids."

A snort escaped Kieran. "Doctors are wrong literally every day, and birth control needs to be taken at the same time each day to truly be effective. When have you seen Mara do anything at the same time every day? She wants breakfast at noon and lunch at four. Not to mention, I've never seen an actor or actress who got to the set on time. My guess is she doesn't remember to take them half the time. She's too busy trying to remember her lines." He could tell by Cal's face he knew Kieran was right. Kieran glanced Henley's way again. "See? He didn't need that to be his first reaction in front of Mara. Mara shouldn't have had to explain that." Kieran's gaze found Cal's once again. A huge smile stretched the man's lips.

Henley groaned. "See? He's happy. We just screwed Mara out of seeing this."

"He can pretend he heard it from her first," Kieran argued, facing Henley once more. "It's not like he won't still be happy when he sees her. Why are you happy?" Kieran asked, his gaze swinging back Cal's way. "I expected there to be a lot of drama and moaning about how you're not fit to parent a child."

"I'm not fit to parent a child," Cal said, still smiling and making Kieran wonder if Cal had snapped. "But Mara is," he said, his smile somehow getting brighter. Cal shrugged. "I never thought I'd get to have any of this—Mara or kids. Those were just more things stolen from me." He laughed, doubling Kieran's fears about his mental health. "It's Mara, you know? I don't know what is it about her, but the rules of nature don't apply to her. I can't stand to be touched, but she doesn't bother me. Supposedly, I can't have kids, yet I am with her. It's just... her. I shouldn't be surprised at all."

"Damn," Kieran cursed under his breath. Henley was right. "I did steal this from Mara."

"Told you so," Henley called from the corner.

Cal stood. "No, you didn't steal anything. I won't let that happen. Thanks for letting me know," Cal said, heading for the door without a backward glance. Kieran watched him go, hoping he hadn't totally ruined his friendship with Mara.

Henley's hands landed on his shoulders, making Kieran jump. He hadn't heard the man move, and he shouldn't be up at all. "You did a good thing," Henley said, leaning down and touching his lips to the spot below Kieran's ear.

"I hope you're right," Kieran said, coming to his feet. "Come on, baby. Let's get you to bed. You shouldn't be on that leg."

"Will you kiss it and make it better?"

"Always," Kieran swore as he helped Henley to the bedroom. He'd never meant anything more. For the rest of his days, he'd kiss Henley and do whatever it took to keep him healthy.

CAL TRIED PRACTICING his speech in his head on the way to Mara's. His nervousness kept him from remembering what he planned to say. Each time he started the speech over, it changed. He'd never been more scared of getting turned away by anyone. The hurt she'd tried hiding, when he'd told her he needed to think, wouldn't leave him. What if he'd fucked things up for good? They were having a baby. Holy shit. Cal almost pulled to the side of the road to put his head between his legs at the thought. He wouldn't leave her alone with that. He wasn't that type of guy. Before he'd gotten the news, he'd already been intent on winning her back, but he didn't know how. Now, it didn't fucking matter how. She would never get rid of him.

By the time Mara's house came in to view, he thought he'd scream from the pressure building inside him. He was in less control than he'd ever been. That was what Mara did to him. His truck hadn't fully stopped running when he jumped from the vehicle, intent on finding Mara. His knuckles barely skimmed the door when it flew open. Michael stood on the other side, staring down at his phone.

"Mara isn't here."

"Where is she?" Cal asked, skipping all the niceties since he didn't have the patience for good manners and Michael didn't expect them.

"Out of town." He started to close the door.

Cal slapped his hand against the wood. "Out of town, where?"

Even with a pissed off Cal hovering over him, Michael didn't look up from his phone. "She went to stay with Chase in the mountains."

Cal tried biting back his irritation. "Could you be a little more specific?"

"I'm sure I could," Michael said, attempting to close the door once more.

Something inside Cal snapped. He grabbed Michael's phone and chucked it. Michael's gaze followed the device across the room, where it hit the wall before slamming to the floor and separating into two pieces. "Do you think you could find me the fucking address?" Cal asked between clenched teeth.

Michael met his gaze. He didn't look put out or angry in any way. Instead, he reached behind him and pulled a second phone from his pocket. "Lucky for you, I have another phone. Otherwise, I wouldn't have been able to pull up the address for you."

Cal bit back a growl. "Thanks, Michael. Sorry about the phone," Cal reluctantly grumbled since he felt like an ass.

"It's 1011 Sasquancha Lane in Sevierville, Tennessee. I'll text you the directions."

Cal's shoulders fell. He probably wouldn't get there until—at least—tomorrow. He hated waiting when something was this important. "Thanks again, and I really am sorry about the phone. Just let me know how much I owe you and I'll buy you a new one."

To his surprise, Michael met his gaze. The man's intensity was almost overwhelming when he focused on anything other than his work. "Don't worry about it. Mara deserves someone who'll show that much passion on her behalf." He shrugged. "Besides, spineless people are boring. I'll book you a flight and car," Michael said before shutting the door in his face.

TWO WEEKS with Chase and Seb had been just what Mara needed. It wasn't the time with friends, relaxation, hiking, or Seb teaching her how to play a first-person shooter game that had given her the perspective she sought. Peace had settled in at some point over the past two weeks. At home, alone, she'd spent too much time overthinking the situation. Yes, Cal had pretty much dumped her days before she learned she was pregnant. And, yes, he'd probably freak the fuck out about the baby once he found out. No matter what, Mara would be okay. She had great friends. That was more than her mother had, and Mara had turned out okay. She also had money and the ability to stay at home. Mara could and would give this child an amazing life. They would be fine alone. That didn't mean her heart didn't hurt, but her life wasn't about her any longer. It was about this tiny miracle that shouldn't be but was. Everything had been stacked against this baby's conception. Yet life had formed anyway. For Mara, it was a lifesaving miracle at the exact moment Cal had decided to break what was left of her. She wasn't angry. Mara didn't hate him. It was her fault for not listening all the times he'd told her he wouldn't heal. She'd loved every broken piece of him, but she failed at making him see that. Now she had other priorities.

"I think I'll go home tomorrow," Mara said, announcing her plans in the middle of a bloody warehouse shoot out with faceless black-clad military men.

"You're welcome to stay as long as you like," Seb said as he threw a grenade over her character's shoulder, helping to clear the path. "There's a second wave of soldiers over this hill."

Mara shifted her weight, leaning closer to the TV in anticipation of another attack. "I appreciate the offer. Chase and you need your privacy, and I've intruded long enough." Having conversations while focusing on a video game made heavy topics easier. "Plus, I guess it's time I stopped hiding."

"You're not hiding," Seb said, easing her pride. "Chase and I are hiding," he said with a low laugh that was sexy enough to make Mara jealous of Chase. Her best friend had the best taste. "Sometimes, you just need to get away and remind yourself how fake the rest of the world is, so you can figure out how to be true to yourself again."

That was exactly what it was like. Mara's situation was a bit different from Chase and Seb's, but not by much. The pair were in the spotlight every bit as much as her. They were hiding now, because they weren't hiding anymore. Not only had Chase finally publicly come out, he'd announced his marriage to Seb—his ex-step-brother. It hadn't been as big of deal as she'd expected. Still, they'd decided to retreat to their cabin in the mountains. They didn't care what anyone thought about their relationship. That didn't mean they wanted to listen to everyone's thoughts.

They completed another level. "I don't know why this game is so oddly satisfying to me."

"Probably because you get to picture you're shooting me."

Mara's head whipped around so fast she almost gave herself whiplash. Cal stood in the doorway of the den with his hands clasped in front of him, looking like the darkest of angels.

"Um, Cal's here," Chase said a little too late behind him, sounding guilty.

"Thanks, Chase." The words came out in a choked whisper. Her throat swelled to the point of painful. "What are you doing here?" She hadn't been ready to see him. Not by a long shot. All the inner pep talks and lectures hadn't prepared her for shit. Fuck him, he was wearing jeans and a long-sleeve t-shirt, making her want to jump him right then. The problem was she wasn't sure if she wanted to fuck him or kick his ass.

"I came for you."

Seb stood. "Well, I'm out. Come on, Chase. Let's go do... something."

Chase nodded, but his gaze slid her way, silently checking with her.

Mara waved him away. "It's fine."

Seb and Chase disappeared, leaving her alone with the missing pieces of her soul. "I'm surprised Chase let you in the door," Mara said, because every other thought she had hurt.

"I convinced him."

"Convincing him better not have included threatening him."

Cal's mouth turned up in one corner. "No. I asked him

if he remembered what happened to that handbag you used to have."

Tears pressed against the backs of Mara's eyes. Of course Chase would let him in after that. Only someone Mara loved would know that story. Only someone who cared about her would remember it. "Did he remember?"

Cal nodded. He looked so damn solemn it hurt her heart. "He said he still has it."

A surprised-sounding snort escaped Mara. "Bitch. He stole my purse."

Even though Cal wasn't smiling, there was laughter in his eyes. There was something else she couldn't name as well. "You ran away."

"You said you needed time to think," Mara shot back.

"It was like an hour and then I was calling myself a dumbass for leaving."

The invisible weight sitting on Mara's chest increased. "You didn't come back."

Cal's gorgeous smile appeared. "Well, then, for about another week, I decided you deserved better than a dumbass."

Mara wanted to run into his arms, but she was scared. "What happened after a week?"

"It turns out even dumbasses have people they can't live without. You're my person. I know you deserve better, but I'm the one who loves you the most."

"I'm pregnant." God help her, the words fell from her lips with no insight from her brain. She just couldn't let him say another word without knowing the whole of it.

Cal's chest expanded as he took a deep breath, and his eyes filled with tears. "Every time I think you can't give me more, you do." Cal's voice broke on the final word and Mara lost the battle against her tears. He still hadn't moved closer, and her body was ready to snap. Even though she knew there'd been other times in her life when she'd thought she'd die from needing someone to hold her, Mara couldn't see past this time right now. But they would have a child soon; she had to be strong.

"If you think there's any chance you'll leave again, do it now. My daddy left, and..." Mara shrugged, incapable of finding the words for that part of her that would always be missing. "I just need you to do it now, if you're going to do it."

Cal shook his head. "You'll have to kill me if you want me to go. It feels like I'm dying already."

"Why?" Mara didn't know why she couldn't stop digging and pushing, but—even if Cal wasn't whole—she needed every little broken piece of him to belong to her.

"Because I love you," Cal said, as if it was the simplest thing in the world. "And I'm not sure if you'll ever let me any closer than I am right now." He visibly swallowed. "I don't know how to live with that."

Mara stood. She swiped at her cheeks as she circled the couch. "Do you mean closer than this?" she asked, moving to stand toe to toe with him.

He nodded. There was hope in his gaze. Hell would freeze before she'd watch it die.

Her hands found his waist. His lips parted as if that small touch set him on fire. "I'm closer already. Seems your fears aren't valid."

"I don't know," Cal said, his voice sounding gravelly. "You haven't kissed me yet."

"I'm not that tall."

Cal bent slightly—just enough she could reach his lips if she stood on her toes. She bit back a laugh. His usual cold demeanor hadn't changed at all, but she knew him now.

This was his teasing side. "I don't know," Mara said, trying to sound put-out. "You're still really—" The air left her lungs as Cal hauled her against him and covered her mouth with his.

Mara's heart twisted in her chest. She'd been so damned scared she'd never feel his kiss again. As much as she tried to deny it to herself, Mara loved him. She couldn't stop touching him, smoothing her hands down his back and stroking his face. Their kiss softened. Mara couldn't completely pull away even though she had things to say.

"So you already knew about the baby, huh?"

"I'm sorry," Cal said, still trying to kiss her. "Blame Kieran."

"It's okay. You obviously came for me when you found out. That says more to me than any words could."

Cal pulled away and set his forehead on Mara's "I came because I love you. Our baby is a bonus."

For a broken man, he'd said the words so easily. As if loving her was understood. He'd also said it twice. Cal deserved to hear them too. "I love you too."

Cal sucked in an audible breath, as if he hadn't breathed while waiting to hear his words returned. "Will you be upset if I skip getting to know your friends today? I'd really like to find a place where I can hold you."

"Do you fish?" Mara asked, rescuing him the same way he'd rescued her in Georgia.

A small smile hovered on Cal's lips. "As a matter of fact, I once caught a shark that almost ate us before we kicked it back overboard."

He had so many sides she hadn't seen and stories she hadn't heard. Mara wanted them all. "Chase has a boat." Mara paused before adding, "There's a bed onboard."

Cal nodded, looking thoughtful. "We should see if he'd loan it to us."

"We should," Mara agreed. They'd only missed a couple of weeks of being together. Mara didn't want to lose another second of his time. They had things to discuss, plans to make, and a life to plan.

CHAPTER ELEVEN

While pushing a thumbtack into the wall, hoping the blue "Baby Shower" sign would stop falling, Cal watched Michael cast his tenth dirty look at a dark-haired guy across the room.

"What's your problem with that guy?"

Michael tried rearranging his features. It was too late for all that. Cal had been watching the drama since Mara's shower started an hour earlier. Since Mara had zero female friends, Chase had gotten all the guys together to throw her a shower. That was probably why none of the decorations would stay put. Chase wouldn't let them use duct tape.

Michael cast another dark look the guy's way. "He used to be my older brother's best friend in high school."

"Okay," Cal said, even more confused.

Michael met his gaze and shrugged. "He was an asshole back then and nothing has changed."

"Ah," Cal said, still not understanding. "I thought you didn't care if people were nice."

As if he couldn't help himself, Michael shot the guy another eat-shit-and-die look. "Sometimes, it matters."

"Why are the two of you whispering together in the corner?" Mara asked as she came to join them.

"Trying to figure out how to get this damn sign to stay," Cal said, hugging her to his side. Mara had already been the most beautiful woman he'd ever seen. Pregnancy enhanced her natural glow. He couldn't stop touching her.

Mara glanced up. "Looks like you finally found a thumbtack. That'll hold it."

"Why is everyone hanging out over here?" Kieran asked as Henley and he joined them.

"Apparently, we're discussing the hanging of decorations."

Both men glanced up. Henley was the first to respond. "Chase wouldn't let us use duct tape."

Obviously, overhearing them, Chase joined in. "You don't want to ruin the paint in your living room. Plus, it would've looked trashy."

"Once again, I disagree," Henley said, picking up the same argument the pair had while decorating earlier. "If their paint can't handle a little duct tape, it'll never handle twin boys."

"I have to agree with my husband," Kieran said, wandering away with everyone else, still bickering. "Gannon and I were hell on our parents' house."

Michael was right there with him. "My twin Marshall and I used to tear our house apart."

"That's true," Gavin said, making Michael shoot him another dirty look. "I was always right there with them."

Cal tuned them out and stared at the wife he never thought he'd have. She was weeks away from giving him two sons. Fuck, no matter how many times he turned it over in his head, Cal couldn't wrap his brain around it. "I love you," he said, because he could never say it often enough. He wondered sometimes if she got sick of hearing it or if she thought he said those words because he didn't have anything else to say. The truth was, he needed her to understand those three words had to cover all the emotions that overwhelmed him every second of every day, because of her. He didn't feel anything else except love, and it was due to her. Everything that he'd suffered was muted in the back of his mind, bearable now, because she'd pushed her way inside his brain, sat down, and refused to budge. He'd told he'd thirty times today already how much he loved her. Chances were good, he'd tell her fifty more. All for one thing...

"I love you too."

This was heaven.

KEEP an eye out for Michael's book, *Clash*.

Characters in this book you might have missed: Gannon and Alex: *Shatter*.

Kieran and Henley: *Thrash*.

Chase and Seb: *Sordid*.

Thanks for sticking with me. If you enjoyed this story, please consider leaving a review on Amazon. It really helps and makes my day.

ABOUT THE AUTHOR

Charity Parkerson is an award winning and multi-published author with several companies. Born with no filter from her brain to her mouth, she decided to take this odd quirk and insert it in her characters.

*Seven-time Readers' Favorite Award Winner
   *2015 Passionate Plume Award Finalist
   *2013 Reviewers' Choice Award Winner
   *2012 ARRA Finalist for Favorite Paranormal Romance
   *Five-time winner of The Mistress of the Darkpath

Connect with her online:

--Join   my   street   team:
facebook.com/TeamCharityParkerson
   --Sign up for my newsletter: http://bit.ly/CharityNews
   --Website: charityparkerson.com
   --Facebook: facebook.com/authorCharityParkerson
facebook.com/TheMenofSin
   --Twitter: twitter.com/CharityParkerso

www.ingramcontent.com/pod-product-compliance
Lightning Source LLC
Chambersburg PA
CBHW060352180626
46817CB00008B/2974